"So, what have yo morning? I've seen you using your crowbar and hammer," she said in an attempt to change the subject.

"I've been removing some of the rotten wood across the front. With those gone, I can then start replacing the rotten wallboard underneath. What's your favorite color?"

She sat back in her chair. "Pink. What's yours?" she asked. The man was positively incorrigible.

"Blue. What's your favorite kind of food?" He bit into one of the cookies and washed it down with a sip of coffee.

"I like all kinds of food, but Mexican is probably my favorite. What's your favorite?"

"Burgers. I love a big, juicy cheeseburger with a side of fries."

"Are you going to ask me what my sign is now? I'm a Libra and as stubborn as you seem, I would guess you're a Taurus. Why are you asking me all of this?"

He tilted his head slightly and the dimple danced in his cheek as he grinned. "I like to learn as much as I can about the woman I'm going to date."

Dear Reader,

Winter is here and as the snow flies, we all seek our own little pocket of warmth in the world. My little pocket is a recliner chair with a soft, furry blanket and a good book. The blanket warms my body, but a good book heats up my very soul.

I hope you find *Guarding a Forbidden Love* to be your heat for a few hours of pleasure. I had a lot of fun writing this one about a middle-aged woman and a sexy younger hunk. I hope Harper and Sam can convince you that love is love and age really doesn't matter.

Enjoy reading!

Carla Cassidy

GUARDING A FORBIDDEN LOVE

Carla Cassidy

HARLEQUIN
ROMANTIC
SUSPENSE

HARLEQUIN®
ROMANTIC SUSPENSE™

Recycling programs for this product may not exist in your area.

ISBN-13: 978-1-335-73823-3

Guarding a Forbidden Love

Copyright © 2023 by Carla Bracale

For questions and comments about the quality of this book, please contact us at CustomerService@Harlequin.com.

Harlequin Enterprises ULC
22 Adelaide St. West, 41st Floor
Toronto, Ontario M5H 4E3, Canada
www.Harlequin.com

Printed in U.S.A.

Carla Cassidy is an award-winning, *New York Times* bestselling author who has written over a hundred and seventy books, including a hundred and fifty for Harlequin. She has won the Centennial Award from Romance Writers of America. Most recently she won the 2019 Write Touch Readers Award for her Harlequin Intrigue title *Desperate Strangers*. Carla believes the only thing better than curling up with a good book is sitting down at the computer with a good story to write.

Books by Carla Cassidy

Harlequin Romantic Suspense

The Scarecrow Murders

Killer in the Heartland
Guarding a Forbidden Love

Colton 911: Chicago

Colton 911: Guardian in the Storm

Cowboys of Holiday Ranch

Sheltered by the Cowboy
Guardian Cowboy
Cowboy Defender
Cowboy's Vow to Protect
The Cowboy's Targeted Bride
The Last Cowboy Standing

Colton 911

Colton 911: Target in Jeopardy

Visit the Author Profile page at Harlequin.com for more titles.

To Darlene, the daughter of my heart. I love being your mother. You make me laugh and you make me proud. I love you...more!

Chapter 1

Harper Brennan sat on her sofa and stared at the birthday cake in the center of her coffee table. The cake was a beautiful dark chocolate, frosted with a rich raspberry buttercream and baked in her very own bakery, the Sweet Tooth.

She'd planned a very small birthday party for herself this evening with two of her best friends. Unfortunately, they had both canceled at the last minute. So now Harper was having a pity party for one and she was the guest of honor.

She grabbed one of the silly pointed party hats she'd bought for the occasion and fastened it atop her head. She then stared at the single candle in the center of the cake. There was only one because there was no way the cake could hold forty-five candles.

Forty-five. She'd never dreamed at this age she would be celebrating a birthday all alone. A little over six years ago, she'd been happily married and had dreamed of opening her own bakery.

She'd managed to see her dream of the bakery come true, but her marriage had ended when her husband had left her for a twenty-five-year-old woman. Jerk. At least the happy couple had moved away so Harper didn't have to see them together every day.

She now sighed and picked up a lighter to light the single candle. In the mood she was in, she felt like bingeing on the cake and eating half of it or more. But she'd only eat a small piece because lately it seemed she only had to look at food and extra pounds jumped right to her tummy and hips. Damn middle age.

Before she could light the candle, a knock sounded at her door. Maybe one of her friends had made it after all. She jumped up off the sofa and hurried to the front door. She opened it to see Sam Bravano standing on her front porch.

"Hi, Harper. I'm here about the ad." He smiled, revealing a dimple in one cheek.

Sam Bravano. She'd seen him around town many times, but nothing had prepared her for seeing him so up close and personal.

Lordy, if she were ten years younger, she would

so jump his bones. And fine bones they were. With his broad shoulders and slim hips, and his slightly shaggy dark hair and his unexpected, yet vivid green eyes, he was definitely a piece of hunky eye candy.

"Harper?" His smile faltered and she realized she'd just been standing there staring at him and maybe mentally drooling a bit. God, she hoped she hadn't really been drooling.

"Oh, yes…the ad. Uh, come on in." She opened the door wider to allow him entry. As he passed by her, she caught the scent of sunshine, a hint of a spicy cologne and intoxicating male.

"Please, have a seat." She gestured him to the chair facing the sofa.

"It's your birthday?" he asked as he sat.

"It is. Would you like a piece of cake? I'd planned a little party for myself with a couple of friends, but at the last minute they couldn't make it."

"That's a shame. It's no fun to celebrate your birthday all alone." He stood, and to her utter surprise, he grabbed one of the party hats from the coffee table and put it on his head.

Even the silly hat didn't detract from his attractiveness.

The man definitely knew how to wear a pair of worn jeans and a T-shirt. His skin was nicely tanned and overall, he just looked incredibly fit.

Harper sank back down on the sofa. "I was just

about to light the candle when you knocked on the door."

"Then by all means, light the candle," he replied and that charming dimple winked at her once again. "How many other candles should there be?"

She laughed. "Enough to burn this house down." She lit the candle.

"Now, wait to blow it out," Sam said. "What's supposed to happen now is everyone sings 'Happy Birthday.' So, here goes…" to her surprise again, he stood up and began to sing the traditional song.

His lovely baritone not only filled the room, but shot a rivulet of warmth straight through her. She swallowed against unexpected tears that burned at her eyes. He was obviously being very kind to a lonely older woman.

"Now, make a good wish and blow out your candle," he said when he finished singing.

She made her wish and blew. "You can take off that silly hat now," she said as she took off the one on her head and set it aside. She picked up the cake server, cut a liberal piece, placed it on one of the decorative plates and then held it out toward him.

He swept the hat off his head and took the cake. "Wow, this looks delicious."

"I hope it is." She handed him a fork.

"Aren't you having a piece?" he asked.

"I'll, uh, have one later. You said you were here about the ad. Sam, I know your work around town and I know you've seen my storefront. It obviously needs a lot of work."

She'd gotten an amazing price on the piece of real estate on Main Street because it had needed a lot of cosmetic work and the mortgage company was eager to sell after the last owner had defaulted on their loan years before.

Since opening the business a little over two years ago she'd focused most of her work and finances on the inside. Now she had enough money saved and a small loan in place to begin the necessary work on the outside.

She'd placed an ad in the local *Millsville News* requesting a carpenter. Sam and his two brothers were all carpenters who often worked at one project or another around town. However, they weren't the only carpenters in town.

"It just needs a bit of a face-lift," Sam now replied.

Yeah, that makes two of us, she thought wryly. "I'd like to do a bit more than a face-lift in the back." As she told him her plans, he set aside his half-eaten cake and pulled out a notepad and pen from his back pocket and began to make notes. He also asked her some questions to clarify exactly what she wanted.

She was acutely aware of him. She'd had men in her living room before, but none of them had filled the space quite like he did. Even sitting, energy wafted from him. It wasn't an uncomfortable energy, rather it was soft and soothing and would instantly put a person at ease.

And yet she felt oddly on edge. Maybe it was because of the way he looked at her so intently, like what she said was the most important thing in the world. Or maybe it was because he exuded a self-confidence and strength in a quiet way. Then there was that dimple…

Oh, the young ladies in town must be positively mad about Sam.

"Business must be good for you to plan all these renovations," he said. He picked up his piece of cake once again.

"It helps to be the only bakery in town," she replied.

"There is that," he agreed with a grin. "But from what I've heard, you're good at what you do. And if this cake is any indication, you're damn good at what you do."

She felt a blush warm her cheeks. "Thanks."

"Did you always want to be a baker?"

The personal question surprised her. "From the time I was a little girl, I liked to bake and dreamed of having a place where I could sell my goodies to other people. My mom loved to bake, too, and we often worked together in the kitchen."

A quick wave of sadness fluttered through her. She'd lost her mother a little over a year before to a heart attack. It was three years after her father had passed away from the same ailment.

"Did you always want to be a carpenter?" she asked in an effort to stave off her sad thoughts.

"My dad was a carpenter all his life and I often went to jobs with him. I wanted to follow in his footsteps. Besides, I enjoy working hard and then seeing something tangible. I enjoy building something new, or rebuilding something old." He laughed. "And that was probably more than you wanted to hear."

"Not at all," she protested. "I've always been interested in what people do and why." She shrugged and felt a blush once again heat her cheeks. "I guess I've always been a people person."

"That's a good thing considering your business, right?" He smiled at her.

"Yes, I suppose it's a good thing," she agreed. She held his gaze for a long moment and then looked down at the cake. "So, what happens now?" She gazed at him once again.

"What I'd like to do is come to the bakery tomorrow morning and take some measurements and check things out. It's the only way I can give you a close estimate as to what all this is going to cost," he replied. "Will nine o'clock work for you?"

"That would be just fine," she agreed.

He stood. "I would encourage you to get several estimates, but I'm betting I can beat anyone else's price and I definitely do better work than anyone else in town." His green eyes sparkled brightly at his last words.

She got up as well and walked with him to the front door. He was a tall drink of water and towered over her shorter frame. She opened the door and then gazed up at him. "Thank you, Sam, for sharing my birthday with me."

He smiled. "It was my pleasure, Harper. I'll see you tomorrow."

Good Lordy, the man looked every bit as good going as he had coming. When he reached his pickup truck in the driveway, she closed her door and locked it.

As she carried the cake and then the dirty dishes to the kitchen, she thought about Sam's suggestion that she get estimates from other places. She didn't intend to waste her time.

She'd already spoken to several people who'd had work done by Sam and his brothers, and everyone had said they were hardworking, delivered on time and had been very fair with their prices. So, why get other estimates?

The only reason she'd placed the ad in the paper was because she had been afraid that Sam and his brothers would already be tied up with other jobs.

She sat at the kitchen table with a small slice of cake before her. It was a slow time at the bakery right now. Fourth of July had passed and the next big holiday was still a couple of months away. Thank goodness she had regular customers who came in daily for coffee and a cinnamon roll, a slice of cake or cookies.

Her birthday cake was delicious and once she'd put it into the refrigerator, she headed for her bedroom even though it was relatively early. Bedtime always came early for her because she tried to be in the bakery by five in the mornings.

Once she was in bed, she couldn't help but think about Sam. He seemed like a nice guy. She guessed he was around thirty years old. Too bad he wasn't, at the very least, ten years older, although even then he would be far out of her league.

She turned over on her back and stared up at the ceiling where moonlight danced in and created flickering shadows. She wouldn't mind having a man in her life again. She missed eating dinner with somebody. She missed intriguing conversations and laughter. She missed watching something as simple as a sunrise or a sunset with a special somebody.

She finally fell asleep and into totally inappropriate and delicious dreams of Sam Bravano.

Sam whistled a cheerful tune as he left Harper's place. The cake was still a delicious taste in his mouth and the woman who had baked it intrigued him.

Harper was a cute little thing with short, curly dark hair and bright blue eyes. She had captured his attention more than once, whenever he saw her out and about in town, although he knew little about her. All he really knew was she had been divorced years ago and owned the bakery.

It had definitely been kind of pathetic to walk in on her having a birthday party all alone. She'd looked charming even with the silly party hat atop her curls. He had no idea what had possessed him to sing to her. He didn't normally do things like that but it had just felt like the right thing to do in the moment.

He pulled away from her house and headed home. As he drove down the main drag of the small town of Millsville, Kansas, a sense of enormous pride filled him. He loved this town and he had worked on several of the storefronts, transforming them from old and tired facades to colorful places that breathed of new life.

He wasn't surprised when he pulled up in his driveway to see his two younger brothers lounging in the two wicker chairs on the front porch. Tony and Michael almost looked like twins despite there being almost two years' age difference between them.

They both had the Bravano dark hair and brown eyes. Sam had no idea where he'd gotten his green eyes from. His father had joked that the mailman had bright green eyes, but there was no doubt that Sam was his father's son. He looked just like his father where Tony and Michael favored their mother. The two brothers sat up straighter in the chairs as he pulled into the driveway.

Sam had bought the two-story house a year ago. He'd gotten a good price for it because it had needed a lot of work and the former owners had just wanted out. His idea was to get it back into good shape and either remain in it or flip it, depending on what the housing market was doing when he got it all finished.

Because his two brothers still lived at home with their mother, they often popped in at his house in the evenings to drink a few beers and shoot the breeze.

Tony wasn't dating anyone in particular at the moment and Michael had an on-again-off-again with his girlfriend named Paula.

"Good evening, boys," he said as he approached them.

"Hey, Sam," Tony said and got up from his chair.

"Where have you been?" Michael asked, also rising from the chair.

"Since when do I need to check in with you?" Sam asked good-naturedly as he unlocked his front door.

"Just wondering, that's all," Michael replied as he and Tony followed Sam through the front door. Tony beelined directly into the kitchen and reappeared a moment later with three beers in hand.

He tossed one to Michael, who had reseated himself on Sam's sofa, and then one to Sam, who then eased down in his recliner. "So, what's new?" Sam asked once they were all seated with their beers cracked open.

"Paula and I broke up again last night," Michael said mournfully.

"Have you ever considered that maybe she's not the right one for you?" Sam asked.

"But I'm crazy about her," Michael lamented.

"You're a schmuck," Tony said. "That girl leads you around like a puppy dog. When she snaps her fingers, you jump. You need to get better game, bro."

"What he needs is a better girlfriend," Sam observed.

"I love Paula. I just need to figure out what she really wants from me," Michael replied. "Once I figure it out, we'll be just fine."

As his two brothers complained and moaned about their love lives or lack thereof, Sam silently sipped his beer. Sam was ten years older than Michael and eight years older than Tony.

At thirty-three years old, Sam had been through the romance wringer. He'd dated a lot of women, but hadn't yet found that special someone. Lately, he felt a quiet desperation wafting from the women he dated. It was the desperation to get married and have babies before time passed them by.

While Sam would love to find a woman who would want to share his life with him, he'd never really wanted children and he wasn't even sure the whole marriage thing was right for him.

Of course, his mother was on him all the time about giving her grandbabies, but he figured his brothers or his older sister, Lauren, could fulfill that wish for their mother.

"So, really…where were you this evening, Sam?" Michael asked again when the conversation about their love lives had finally waned.

"I answered Harper Brennan's ad in the paper for a carpenter. She wants to have a little work done at the Sweet Tooth," Sam replied.

"Does that mean we all have a new job?" Tony asked. "We've still got to finish up the gazebo in the town square." Several weeks ago, the members of the town council had hired them to build a gazebo that people in town could enjoy.

"There isn't that much left to do on that job. I figure you two, along with Bud and Aaron, can finish things up there," Sam replied. Bud Kurtz and Aaron Palmer were a couple of teenagers who were always up to earn extra money by working for the Bravano brothers.

"What exactly does Harper want done?" Tony asked.

"I'm not exactly sure. I'm meeting her in the morning to discuss the specifics. From what little she already told me I should be able to handle a lot of it on my own. However, I'll need you two to help me there in a few weeks or so," Sam said.

He found it odd that for some reason he was reluctant to share with his brothers too much about his time spent with Harper this evening. He also found it odd that he was also reluctant to have them working with him there, at least initially.

"Have you heard if Dallas has any more clues in Cindy's murder?" Tony asked, changing the subject.

"That was creepy as hell," Michael said darkly.

"As far as I've heard he's no closer to finding her murderer," Sam replied.

It had been a little over a month since the body of Cindy Perry, a young woman who had worked as a waitress at the local café, had been found in Lucas Maddox's cornfield.

She'd been trussed up to a pole like a human scarecrow. She'd been stabbed to death and, according to local gossip, her mouth had been sewn shut with thick black thread and her eyes had been missing.

Dallas Calloway, the chief of police, had quickly let it be known that Lucas wasn't a suspect in the murder. Unfortunately as far as Sam had heard, there didn't seem to be any viable suspects. The murder had definitely cast a pall over the whole town.

"It's got to be somebody Cindy made mad," Tony said.

"The person who did that to her was more than mad," Michael added darkly. "It was somebody who was sick to do those things to her.

Thankfully his brothers didn't stay too long after that and the next morning at quarter 'til nine, he pulled up and parked in front of the Sweet Tooth Bakery.

The bakery was in a good location on Main Street, and Harper's house was just a little over a block away. The commercial building had rotting boards and was painted a fading, tired brown. The only saving grace was the large bright pink sign that hung over the doorway. It not only had the name of the place on it, but also an illustration of a cupcake with white icing and pink sprinkles.

The sign could remain, but most all of the wood on the front either needed to be replaced or painted. The air just outside of the building smelled absolutely mouthwatering.

He'd never been inside the business before even though he enjoyed cakes and cookies and such as much as the next person. But his mother baked goodies regularly so he'd never felt the need to go into the bakery.

He opened the front door and stepped inside. In here the scents were even more delicious. Directly ahead of him was a long glass display case holding beautiful cakes, cupcakes and a variety of other sweets. A coffee machine was behind the counter, one of those fancy ones that spewed out straight coffee or cappuccino or hot chocolate.

There were several high round-topped glass tables with pink-and-white-striped chairs. The walls were white with pink trim and there were several large photos on them depicting cakes he assumed Harper had baked. Harper was nowhere to be seen but there was a bell on the counter and so he rang it.

She came through a doorway that led to the back. She was clad in a pair of jeans that hugged her slender legs and a blue blouse that did amazing things to her blue eyes. Over it all, she had on a blue-and-white apron that sported a bit of flour.

"Sam, I'm sorry, I didn't hear you come in," she said with a smile.

"It's okay. I've just been looking around. It's quite inviting in here."

"Thanks. It's a total disconnect with the outside, right?"

"Right, but we're going to fix that," he said confidently. "We'll make sure the outside is as inviting as the inside."

"That's the plan," she agreed with a wide smile that lit up her entire face.

"I just wanted to let you know I was here and that I'll be outside doing some measuring and then later I'll come back in and give you an estimate."

"That sounds perfect to me," she agreed. "I'm really looking forward to getting the process started." Her eyes sparkled brightly. God, she had pretty eyes with long dark lashes.

"Then I'll see you back in here in about twenty minutes." With a smile, he turned and walked out of the shop. He whistled as he walked back to his truck and retrieved his tape measure and a small pad and pen.

Before he could start measuring, Joe Rogers approached the shop. "Hey, Joe. How's life?" Sam greeted. Sam would guess that Joe was in his late fifties or early sixties. He was divorced and lived on a small farm at the edge of town.

"It's going," Joe replied. "Although my days don't really begin until I get a cup of coffee and one of Harper's big cinnamon rolls. Looks like she's finally ready to do something to spruce up the place."

"That's why I'm here," Sam replied. "See you later, Joe, and enjoy your cinnamon roll."

"I always do," the man said and then disappeared into the bakery.

For the next twenty minutes or so, Sam measured and made assessments about what needed to be done and what supplies he would need. He worked enough in the business that he had a rough idea about the cost of lumber and other supplies he would need to buy.

When he was all finished, he reentered the shop. Joe was seated at one of the tables and Harper stood behind her display case. Sam walked up to her. "I'd like a cup of black coffee and one of your cinnamon rolls. Joe led me to believe they must be really good. Then whenever you're ready to talk, I'm ready." He pulled out his wallet.

"Put that away," she said. "It's on the house this morning."

"Is that because you like me?" he teased.

"No… I mean yes…" Her cheeks turned a charming pink. "Why don't you have a seat at one of the tables and I'll be right with you."

"Harper, I'm taking off," Joe said. "I'll see you tomorrow morning."

"Okay, Joe," she replied. "See you tomorrow."

As Joe left, Harper carried the coffee and the cinnamon roll to where Sam sat. She set the things on the table and then took a seat across from him. "So, what have you got for me?"

"This is only an estimate on the front of the building. You'll need to walk out back with me to show me what you want specifically done out there," he explained.

As he went over the supplies and the cost, he was only interrupted once when Letta Lee, president of the gardening club, came in.

Letta was a sixty-something-year-old woman who Sam believed was one of the most judgmental snobs in town. She was also known to be a big gossip. Thankfully, she picked up a cake she'd ordered and then left without speaking to him, which didn't surprise him.

"So, when can you start work?" Harper asked when she rejoined him at the table.

"As soon as you want," he replied.

"As soon as you can," she said.

"I'll draw up a contract for you to sign this afternoon and then I can get started," he replied.

"A contract? Is that really necessary?"

He smiled at her. "It not only protects me, but it protects you as well. So yes, it's necessary." He got up from the table. "I'll be back in about an hour or so with the paperwork."

"I'll be here," she replied.

Two hours later the financial aspect of the job had been hammered out, the contract had been signed and Sam left the bakery once again to head to the lumber yard to arrange for the supplies he would need.

He was eager to get started on the job and he was even more eager to get to know Harper better. For the first time in a long time, a woman interested and attracted him.

He wasn't sure what it was about her, but he felt a spark with her and he couldn't wait to explore it…and her. He would be spending long days working outside her shop, but he'd also make sure he got plenty of opportunities to spend some time inside her shop and engage her on a more intimate basis.

Chapter 2

Harper leaned on her elbows over the display case, her chin in her hands as she watched Sam working outside. She knew it was miserably hot and humid outside and fifteen minutes ago Sam had stripped off his T-shirt. Lordy, just the sight of his bare broad shoulders and six-pack abs made Harper feel hot and humid despite the coolness inside the building.

Earlier that afternoon supplies had been dropped off just to the side of the front door. There were all kinds of lumber and exterior wall boards and everything else needed to transform the outside of the front of the building.

However, at the moment her sole attention was on Sam. He used a crowbar to take off some old wood trim, and as he did, his arm muscles bunched and danced. Oh, but the man was hot.

He suddenly stopped his work and peered into the shop. A slow grin curled his lips and he winked at her. Harper straightened up and looked down into the display case, appalled that he had caught her staring at him.

It had been a slow morning and was winding up to be an equally slow afternoon. Joe had been in earlier for his usual cup of coffee and cinnamon roll. A couple of other regulars had also come in.

Mandy Creighton, a nice lady, had come in to pick up a birthday cake she'd ordered for one of her sons' birthdays. Other than that, it was just too hot outside for people to enjoy walking around and shopping. Harper had a feeling today people were thinking more about crisp salads and cold pasta dishes than baked goodies.

It was around three when Sam entered the shop. He had pulled his T-shirt back on and announced it was break time for him. She hadn't even seen him take a lunch break.

He walked up to the counter with that smile that filled Harper with unexpected heat. Or maybe she was just on the verge of having another one of her hot flashes.

"I'm determined to try all the sweets in here, and I mean all the sweets." His green eyes pierced into hers as another slow smile curved his lips.

Good golly, was he flirting with her? Surely

not. She was old enough to be his…well, not his mother, but his much older sister. "So, what would you like to try today? A slice of cake or some cookies?" She hated that she sounded like a half-breathless schoolgirl.

"I'd think I'd like to try your cookies today," he replied. "A couple of those raisin oatmeal ones. I'd also like a cup of coffee and since nobody else is in here maybe you can sit with me at one of the tables."

"I can do that," she replied.

"Now, how much do I owe you?" he asked.

"It's on the house," she replied.

"No," he said firmly. "We're not doing that. You run a business here and I pay my own way. You should never give away what you work hard to create. Now, how much do I owe you?" he repeated.

She told him and he paid and then she waved him toward the tables. He must want to discuss some of the work outside, she thought. Otherwise, why would he want her to join him? "Go ahead and sit down and I'll be right there."

As he sat, she plated a couple of the big cookies, got his coffee and then joined him at the table. "So, what's up?" she asked.

He frowned. "Nothing's up."

"Then why did you want me to sit with you?" she asked.

"Because I'd like to get to know you better."

She blinked and then stared at him. "Why?"

He laughed, the deep, pleasant sound rolling over her like a warm blanket on a cold day. "Why not? I'm going to be working for you here for a while and besides, I find you very attractive."

His words left her momentarily speechless. "Oh well…uh…we can certainly visit when you take your breaks and there's nobody else in the shop," she finally sputtered.

"Are you dating anyone at the moment?" he asked.

"Uh, no." Once again, he'd caught her off guard.

"Good, I was thinking maybe we could visit even more if I took you out to dinner tonight," he replied.

Once again, she stared at him. Was this some kind of a joke? Maybe he'd made a bet with one of his brothers or some friends that he could get the much older baker woman to fall for him. Or maybe he was just being foolish.

She finally laughed. "You're funny."

"I wasn't trying to be funny. I am being completely serious. I'd like to take you out to dinner at the café. If tonight doesn't work for you then I'm free any other night."

"That sounds like a date and, Sam, there's no way on earth I'm going out on a date with you. The whole idea is positively absurd."

"It's not absurd at all." His eyes twinkled and he leaned forward. "This just means I need to work a lot harder to show you my charm and to entice you to go out with me."

She laughed again. "Good luck with that." She was just grateful that her voice didn't betray the slight breathlessness the whole conversation had caused inside her. The idea of going out on a date with Sam Bravano was wildly appealing, but utterly ridiculous.

"So, what have you been doing this morning? I've seen you using your crowbar and hammer," she said in an attempt to change the subject.

"I've been removing some of the rotten wood across the front. With that gone, I can then start replacing the rotten wallboard underneath. What's your favorite color?"

She sat back in her chair. "Pink. What's yours?" she asked. The man was positively incorrigible.

"Blue. What's your favorite kind of food?" He bit into one of the cookies and washed it down with a sip of coffee.

"I like all kinds of food, but Mexican is probably my favorite. What's your favorite?"

"Burgers. I love a big, juicy cheeseburger with a side of fries."

"Are you going to ask me what my sign is now? I'm a Libra and as stubborn as you seem, I would guess you as a Taurus. Why are you asking me all of this?"

He tilted his head slightly and the dimple danced in his cheek as he grinned. "I like to learn as much as I can about the woman I'm going to date."

She laughed and got up from the table. "You are some piece of work, Sam Bravano."

"Speaking of work, I'd better get back to it." He ate the last bite of cookie and took a drink of the coffee. "Those were the best cookies I've ever tasted."

"Thanks," she replied. "I'm glad you liked them." She watched as he threw his plastic plate and napkin away and then started out the door, but before he could completely leave, he paused and turned back to her. "And just for your information, I'm a Cancer. I love deep and hard and I enjoy taking care of my partner." With that, he left.

She released a deep sigh. It had been fun to spar with him a little bit, and she had to admit his flirting with her had definitely tickled her. It had been a very long time since a man had flirted with her. Even if he'd just been toying with her, she admitted to herself that it had still been fun.

She sighed and picked up a cleaning cloth in an attempt to ignore the man, who was once again shirtless and working just outside her front windows. He was definitely more than a bit of a diversion.

For the rest of the afternoon, she cleaned the display case and all of the tabletops. She kept herself busy so she wasn't caught again just standing and watching Sam. It had been bad enough that he'd caught her staring at him one time.

She gathered up all the cleaning cloths she'd used during the day and carried them through the kitchen and into a small laundry room. She threw them into the washing machine and set it to wash. She went through tons of the cloths in a day and it was wonderfully convenient to have the washer and dryer here.

At quarter 'til four she made a fresh pot of coffee and at four one of her best friends walked into the shop. "I see work has begun," Becky Barlow said as Harper poured them each a cup of the fresh brew.

Becky sank down at one of the tables and Harper carried the coffee to the table and then joined her friend there. Harper and the blond-haired, brown-eyed woman had been friends for years. They'd gone all through school together and had become really close during high school.

Becky was happily married to her high school boyfriend. They had a son and a daughter and they had just enjoyed the birth of their first grandchild. Becky worked as a third-grade teacher at the school and had always been wonderfully supportive of Harper through all her ups and downs.

She now sat facing the window and as Sam passed by, she let out a low whistle and then grinned at Harper. "Nice view," she said.

"Really? I hadn't noticed," Harper replied with pretend airiness.

Becky laughed. "Yeah, right. Harper, I've got news for you. You're divorced, not dead."

"Okay, so maybe I have noticed a little bit," Harper said with a laugh of her own. "In fact, I'll admit the view has been a bit distracting all day."

"No doubt," Becky replied. "If I was ten years younger and single, I swear I'd take that hunky boy to bed and make his head spin."

"Becky." Harper laughed once again. "You're feeling pretty feisty this afternoon."

"I'm just trying to make up for the crummy day I had."

"What made it crummy?" Harper asked curiously.

"Benny McGraw threw up all over the back of Lizzie Dominic and then while Alice Jackson was trying to escape the puke, she slipped and slid and fell right into it. So, math class involved one sick, crying boy and two screaming, crying girls. It took almost an hour to finally get it all sorted out and for the class to calm down again."

Harper couldn't help but laugh at the visual picture Becky had painted. "I'm just sorry I can't offer you anything more than coffee," she said sympathetically. "Sounds like you need something much stronger."

Becky laughed. "It's okay. I'm fine with the coffee. As far as I'm concerned, the day was just an example of how teachers are warriors who tackle short attention spans, crazy parents and puke. By the way, on another subject, I'm really sorry I missed your birthday party."

"It was no big deal," Harper replied even as a vision of Sam sitting in her living room filled her head. She was almost glad now that her two friends hadn't been able to show up.

"So, tell me, what's new with you?" Becky asked and then took a sip of her coffee.

"Not much. I'm really excited about getting the outside of the bakery cleaned up and once that's done, we'll start work on the backyard. I have all kinds of exciting ideas that I want to see back there."

"I think you'll see a big uptick in sales once the outside of the bakery looks just as good as the inside," Becky said.

"From your lips to God's ears," Harper replied.

"People just don't know how nice it is in here by looking at the outside." Becky took another sip of her coffee.

For the next few minutes, the two continued to visit and when the coffee was gone, Becky got up from the table.

"Time for me to get home. Larry told me he was cooking dinner for me tonight and it would be ready by five."

"Lucky you," Harper said, also rising from the

table. "Go enjoy your dinner and tell Larry I said hi. I'll see you sometime next week."

Becky stopped by about once a week or so for a quick cup of coffee after work. She told Harper it was her decompression time before she headed home.

Sometimes their other friend, Allie Crawford, joined them, but her work hours didn't always allow it. However, occasionally the three of them would go out to dinner together.

Once Becky was gone, Harper cleaned the tabletop once again and then poured herself a tall glass of water. If she drank any more coffee, she'd be up half the night. She already had to deal with hot flashes and occasional night sweats that often disrupted her sleep. Perimenopause, the doctor had told her. Early hell as far as Harper was concerned.

At five o'clock she turned the sign on the door from Open to Closed. She went back into the kitchen and made sure everything was clean and ready for the baking she would do the next morning. She switched the cloths from the washer to the dryer, turned it on and then grabbed her purse and walked out the front door.

Sam was in the process of putting his tools away into a large wooden carrier. "Harper, hang on a minute." She stopped in her tracks and then watched as he loaded the carrier into the back of his pickup truck. Then he hurried back to where she stood.

"Now I'm ready," he said with a wide smile.

"Ready for what?" she asked curiously.

"To walk you home," he replied. "I'm assuming you usually walk to and from work."

"Uh…well yes, I do. It seems silly to drive less than two blocks from my house to here. The only times I do drive is if it's raining hard or too cold and snowy. Although sometimes I don't mind walking through the snow. However, I usually enjoy walking instead of driving here."

She shut her mouth, aware that she was rambling. For some reason Sam made her nervous, not in a bad way, but rather in an inexplicable good way.

"So today, if you don't mind, I'd enjoy walking you home." He cast her that smile that made his dimple dance and her knees weaken.

"I guess I don't mind if you don't mind," she replied. She was so confused by him.

What on earth did Sam Bravano really want from her?

They took off down the sidewalk at a leisurely pace. He walked close enough to her that he could smell the scents of sugar and cinnamon and everything sweet. But there was also an underlying fragrance of something hot and spicy. That scent he found exceedingly attractive and it called to something deep inside him.

"You look very pretty today," he said to her. It

was true, the pink blouse she wore enhanced the darkness of her hair and the bright blue of her eyes. The cut of the blouse, along with the skinny black jeans she wore, also showcased her lush body to perfection.

"Thanks," she said, her cheeks dusted with a pink color to rival her blouse.

He found her blushes positively charming. It had been a long time since he'd seen a woman blush. "It looked like a friend came in to visit with you this afternoon," he said.

"Yes, Becky Barlow. She and I have been good friends since we were sophomores in high school. She's a teacher at the elementary school and we've seen each other through a lot of ups and downs over the years. Do you have a best friend?" she asked.

"My best friends are my two brothers, even though they are quite a bit younger than me," he replied. "They're my friends, but since our dad passed away two years ago, I'm also kind of like a father figure to them."

"Oh, I'm so sorry about your father. I lost mine four years ago and then my mother last year," she replied.

He heard the sadness in her and it resonated with a grief in him. His father had been his hero. Anthony Bravano had been bigger than life, a gregarious man who never knew a stranger and who had loved his family fiercely. When he'd died, a huge hole had been left behind not only in the family, but also deep inside Sam's heart.

"Do you have siblings?" he now asked her.

"No, I'm an only child," she replied.

"Sometimes I wish I was," Sam said with a laugh. "So, what do you like to do in your spare time? I know the bakery is closed on Sundays."

"The one thing I don't do on Sundays is bake. I like to do a little gardening and I enjoy reading. Things I'm sure you would find pretty boring."

"Actually, I don't find those things boring at all. I like to do a little gardening, too, although I don't do as much reading as I should," he confessed.

"I imagine you spend a lot of your spare time at Murphy's," she said, naming a popular bar in town.

"Ha, not at all. I outgrew the bar scene a long time ago," he replied. "I haven't been to Murphy's in years."

He saw the disbelief that flashed in her eyes. "Then what do you do in your spare time?"

He was pleased that she was asking questions of him. Surely, that meant she had a little interest in him. "I bought a house last year that needed a lot of work, so that's what I do in my spare time."

"So, you work hard all day long and then go home and work some more," she said. Again, her voice held more than a touch of disbelief.

"Why am I getting the impression that you don't believe me?" he asked.

She stopped walking and turned to face him.

"Sam, a man who looks like you has got to have a…uh…robust social life."

"I'd like to have a social life with you, Harper," he said.

She started walking at a quicker pace. "There you go, being totally ridiculous again."

"I'm not being ridiculous," he protested and quickly caught up with her. "Harper, why can't you believe that I'd like to take you out on a real date?"

By that time, they had reached her front porch. She turned and faced him once again, her beautiful eyes filled with skepticism. "What did you do, Sam? Make a bet with your buddies that you could romance the old lady in the bakeshop? Are your friends waiting to see if you're successful or not? How much money will you get if you succeed?"

"God, no." He was appalled that she would even think such a thing about him. "There's no bet and you aren't the old lady baker. How can you even refer to yourself like that? I see you as a very attractive, lively woman who I'd like to spend more time with."

She unlocked her front door and then turned and looked at him. "Sam, you seem like a very nice young man. Go find somebody your own age to play with."

Before he could reply, she flew into her house and closed the door. Sam stared at the door for a long moment and then turned around and headed back up the sidewalk.

He was more determined than ever to get her to go out with him. He now knew what he was up against. She believed he couldn't possibly be attracted to her because of the age thing.

Well, she was dead wrong. For the first time in a very long time Sam looked forward to seeing and talking to a woman again. He really had no idea exactly what drew him to her, but something was definitely there.

And despite what she said, he thought she was drawn to him, too. If he truly believed she had no interest in him then he would just show up at the bakery and do his job. But his plan right now was to show up there and do his job and try to convince her to go out with him.

He was back to work at eight the next morning when the bakery opened. For the next hour or so, people he assumed were regular customers came and went.

It was another hot and humid day, although not quite as bad as it had been the day before. Just after one there was a lull in the customer traffic and he was ready to take a break inside the cool interior.

He went inside where Harper stood behind the display case. Today she was clad in a pair of black slacks and a bright yellow blouse. She also wore an apron that read Sweet Tooth across the front.

"Afternoon, Harper." He walked up to the counter. She definitely looked like a sweet treat he'd like to savor. There was just something about her that drew him to her. Maybe it was her bright smile or the sparkle in her big blue eyes.

"Hi, Sam."

"You look like a bright ray of sunshine today... a very pretty ray," he said.

He was unsurprised by the faint blush that filled her cheeks. "Thank you. Now, what can I get for you?"

"How about three of those cookies that I like... the oatmeal raisin ones, and a cup of coffee," he said. He pulled some money from his wallet and then watched as she got everything ready for him. "You going to come and sit with me?" he asked once he'd paid.

"Uh...not today. I need to clean some things up back here," she replied, not quite meeting his gaze.

"Okay then," he replied easily. He carried the cookies and his coffee to a table nearest the display counter and sat. "It looked like you were fairly busy this morning." He watched as she began to clean the top of the display case, which he suspected was already clean.

"I think almost all my regulars came in. Then I've got two cakes and two dozen cupcakes going out this afternoon."

"That's good, right?"

"That's about normal for a Friday afternoon," she replied. "There are always parties on the weekends and thankfully people want cakes or cupcakes."

"So, the people in Millsville like their cake."

"Thank goodness for me," she replied with a laugh. He liked the sound of her laughter. It was a musical sound that was quite pleasant to the ears.

"Have you ever considered hiring somebody to help you out here so you aren't working from five or six in the morning until five in the evening six days a week?"

She paused with her cloth in hand. "I've considered it, but I've been saving every penny I can scrape together for the renovations. Once those are all done and paid for then I'll maybe consider hiring another person to work here part-time. Although I have to admit I'm a bit of a control freak and the idea of having somebody else in my kitchen kind of stresses me out."

"That reminds me, maybe right after work today we could go around back and you can tell me exactly what you want done out there," he said.

"That will work," she replied. "I'm eager to show you what I want. I have to warn you, it's going to be a lot."

"Then it's a date," he said with a grin.

"No, Sam, it's not a date. It's a…a…business appointment," she replied.

He laughed. "You are one stubborn woman."

"And you are one tenacious man," she returned with a small grin of her own.

"I just know what I like and when I like something I go after it," he replied. "So, this is a fair warning, Harper Brennan, I intend to do whatever I can to prove to you that I want to date you."

Her eyes sparkled brightly and she laughed. "Just remember I am one stubborn woman and right now I don't see that happening at all."

"Ah, but you haven't seen the full brunt of the Sam Bravano charm yet."

She laughed once again. "At this point in my life, I've got to warn you, I'm pretty immune to charm, Sam."

She might say that now, but she'd cleaned the same spot on the top of the display case three times now. He ate his cookies and finished up his coffee and then headed back outside. Maybe one of the ways to Harper's heart was for him to work hard and give her the storefront she'd always dreamed of.

He knocked off at five o'clock and went into the bakery right before Harper closed for the night. She appeared to be ready for him. Gone was her apron and the minute he was inside she turned the sign on the door to indicate the business was closed and then she locked up.

"We'll go out the back door. I hope you brought your pad and pencil because there are a lot of things I want done out back," she said.

"Got them right here," he said and patted his back pocket.

"Okay then, let's go." There was a lilt to her voice that spoke of her excitement.

He followed her into a pristine kitchen with

commercial-grade equipment. "So, this is where all the magic happens," he said.

"I don't know about magic, but this is where all the work is done," she replied.

"I'm sure it's hard work," he agreed quickly.

She smiled. "It is, but it's work I absolutely love. Let's head outside," she said and led him through the laundry area.

"After you," he said and opened the back door. She walked out before him. She took about three steps out and then froze and suddenly screamed.

Then he saw it…a scarecrow standing in the backyard. However, it wasn't a scarecrow made of corn husks and hay. Rather it was a human scarecrow. He immediately recognized the young woman despite the fact that her mouth was sewn shut with thick black thread and her eyes were missing.

It was Sandy Blackstone, who worked as a teller at the bank. She was dressed in an ill-fitting pair of jeans and a red-and-black plaid shirt, a straw hat set atop her head at a cocky angle. It took only an instant for his mind to process the horrendous sight.

He grabbed the screaming Harper by the shoulders, whirled her around and drew her into his arms, not wanting her to see the horrible scene for a moment longer.

Chapter 3

Harper clung to Sam and was grateful for his big, strong arms holding her tight. She'd finally stopped screaming but now wept uncontrollably into the front of his shirt as the vision of Sandy tied to the pole with her mouth sewn shut and her eyes missing continued to fill her head over and over again. It was positively horrifying.

"You're okay," Sam's deep voice said softly... soothingly. He rubbed her back in small circles, obviously in an attempt to calm her down. "I'm so sorry you had to see that, Harper."

She nodded, her face still buried in the front of his T-shirt as her tears continued to fall. Who would do such a thing? Dear God, who was even capable in this small town of doing such unspeakable things to a pretty young woman?

"Come on, let's go back inside. I need to call Dallas." He gently guided her toward the back door and when they went back into the kitchen, she sank down on the folding chair she kept there.

She tried desperately to pull herself together as Sam made the call to the chief of police. But the vision of Sandy was burned into her brain and caused icy shivers to rush up and down her spine. Along with the horror was the grief of a young woman lost…a young woman dead far before her time. Dear God, who had done those terrible things to Sandy?

Sam hung up his phone, tucked it back into his pocket and then knelt down in front of her. "Are you okay?" he asked. He ran his thumbs down the tear tracks on her cheeks. His touch was infinitely gentle and for some reason made her want to cry all over again. But she swallowed against her tears and nodded.

"I'm okay. But, why here?" She finally managed to say. "Why was she left here, Sam? She's never even been in the bakery before. I only know her from the times she's waited on me at the bank."

"Dallas will sort it all out when he gets here," Sam replied. His beautiful green eyes seemed to reach out and caress her. "I just need to know that you're all right. You've been through one hell of a shock."

"I... I'm okay," she repeated even though it wasn't really true. She was definitely shaken up to her very core and still aghast by what she'd seen. "D-did you know her?" she asked, trying to wrap her mind around everything. "Did you know Sandy?"

"Like you, I only knew her from the bank." He rose to his feet. "We need to go up front to meet Dallas."

She rose and preceded him into the shop, where they both sat at a table near the window to wait for the lawman. "You might want to make a pot of coffee, it's probably going to be a long night," he suggested.

She jumped back up, grateful for something... anything to do, even though nothing could distract her from the horror in her backyard.

Poor Sandy. She'd always found the blonde with her bright blue eyes and wide smiles very pleasant whenever she'd helped Harper at the bank. Why? That was the question that kept racing through her head.

Why had Sandy been killed and why had she been left behind the bakery? It was just like what she'd heard about Cindy Perry being found in Lucas's cornfield. Who was committing these heinous murders of young women?

The coffee had just finished brewing when Dallas and two of his officers showed up. Dallas Calloway was a nice-looking guy with curly black hair and silver-gray eyes. Right now, he looked as grim as she'd ever seen him. Officers Joel Penn and Darryl O'Conner looked just as serious as their boss.

Harper offered the coffee to them, but all the men declined. As Sam told Dallas about them going out to the backyard to look at the building, Harper poured herself a cup of the coffee and returned to her chair. She wrapped her fingers around the warmth of the mug in an effort to heat the iciness that remained deep inside her.

"I've called Josiah so he should be here anytime," Dallas said. Josiah Mills was the town's undertaker and the county coroner. "Is there access to the backyard any other way than besides through here?"

"The yard is fenced, but there's a gate on the east side," she said. "D-do you need me to go back out there and show it to you?" She didn't want to go back there again. She didn't want to see Sandy like that again.

"No," Sam replied quickly. "There's absolutely no reason for you to go back out there. I'm sure we can find the gate without your help."

She smiled at him gratefully. She knew he was trying to protect her. What she wanted right now was to be back in his strong arms. She wanted to bury herself in his scent of sunshine and a faint spicy cologne and forget that there was a dead woman tied to a pole in her backyard.

Instead, he and the rest of the men went out the back door, leaving her alone in the bakery. Dear Lord, this made the second woman who had been killed by the man dubbed the Scarecrow Killer. One murder had been frightening enough, but now with two victims, it was possible…probable that Dallas was dealing with a serial killer. The very idea shot a new wave of horror through her. She'd never dreamed something like this could happen in her small hometown. Things like this happened in big cities, not here in Millsville…at least that was what she'd always believed before now.

Hopefully Dallas would be able to find something…anything that would lead him to an arrest. The killer definitely needed to be behind bars or in a mental institution as soon as possible. Anyone capable of doing something like what had been done to Sandy, and Cindy Perry before her, had to either be mentally ill or just plain evil.

She jumped as a knock sounded on the door. It was Josiah along with his younger assistant, Gary Walters. Josiah was in his mid to late sixties. From what she'd heard about him, when anyone asked him when he intended to retire his reply was always that he'd stop working when he was dead. He occasionally came into the bakery for a dozen cookies or a couple of cupcakes. Harper knew he was a widower and lived on the outskirts of town.

On the other hand, Gary was in his late twenties or early thirties. He was as shy as Josiah was boisterous. He was unassuming with rather drab brown hair and eyes, but he had a beautiful smile.

He'd never been in the bakery before, but Harper had interacted with him and found him very helpful and caring when both of her parents had passed and she'd been grieving.

She quickly unlocked the door and let them in. "Harper, not so good to see you under these inauspicious circumstances," Josiah said.

"Definitely not the best of circumstances," she agreed. "Hi, Gary."

"'Evening, Ms. Harper," he said.

"Dallas and…uh…she's in the backyard," she said and then gestured them on out the back door.

The minutes ticked by and slowly turned into hours. Several times Sam popped in to check on her. Finally, after what seemed like forever, Sam and Dallas came inside and asked for a cup of coffee. She jumped up to serve them and then Dallas gestured her back to her table, where all three of them sat.

"Harper, I need to ask you a few questions," Dallas said. "First of all, did you know Sandy Blackstone outside of her work at the bank?"

"No, she was just a teller who occasionally helped me when I went into the bank, but I didn't know her personally at all," she replied.

"I know you must hear some gossip in here. Have you ever heard about anyone else having a problem with Sandy?" Dallas asked.

She shook her head. "I've never even heard anyone mention her name."

"When was the last time you went out into your backyard?" he asked.

She frowned thoughtfully. "It's been at least a week or so. H-how long has she been out there?"

Sam reached for her hand and she was grateful for the slightly calloused fingers and palm that swallowed her smaller hand in welcomed warmth. "Not long, Harper," he said softly.

A small sense of relief fluttered through her. She would hate to think that poor girl had been in her backyard for days and days without anyone discovering her. It was bad enough she was back there at all.

Dallas only had a few more questions for her and then for Sam. "I have more men coming and we'll probably be in your backyard for at least several more days collecting evidence, but since we can access it through the side gate, you can operate your business in here as usual. You and Sam are now free to go. You can lock up the front and back doors. I'm assuming you'll both be available if I have any more questions."

"Absolutely," she said and Sam echoed her sentiment.

Sam released her hand and she got up from the table. Dallas disappeared out the back door once again and she emptied the last of the coffee and set the machine up for the next morning.

"I'll drive you home," Sam said.

She started to protest, but darkness had fallen outside and suddenly the idea of walking home all alone was abhorrent. Somewhere on the streets of Millsville there was a killer on the loose. "Okay," she agreed. "I appreciate it."

"If you'll give me the key, I'll lock up the back door for you," he said.

Once again, she looked at him gratefully. She didn't want to go back there again. She didn't want another vision of Sandy trussed up like a human scarecrow in her brain and Sam must have known that.

She gave Sam the key and minutes later they walked out the front door and to his truck in the parking lot. His truck interior smelled just like him, of a touch of sunshine and the cologne she found so attractive. She leaned back against the padded seat and watched him walk around to the driver's-side door.

Thank God he'd been with her when she'd stepped out the back door. Thank goodness he'd been there to hold her and comfort her. She would have come completely undone if he hadn't been there for her and she'd had to face that horrible sight all alone.

"I feel like I'm stuck in a very bad dream…like I'm in a horrible nightmare and I can't wake up," she said as he started the truck engine. "I know it's crazy, but I somehow feel guilty…like I've done something terribly wrong. Otherwise, why was she left in my yard?"

"Harper, this had nothing to do with you personally and you did absolutely nothing wrong. This is just like when Cindy Perry was left in Lucas Maddox's cornfield. That had absolutely nothing to do with Lucas. This is some sort of a crazy random thing and you need to stop any thoughts of guilt you might be entertaining."

"That poor woman. She must have suffered so much pain." Tears once again filled her eyes as she thought about Sandy's horrendous ordeal at the hands of her murderer.

"If it's any consolation at all, Josiah said she was already dead from several stab wounds to her abdomen when her mouth was sewn shut and her eyes were removed. Damn, don't tell anyone her eyes were removed. Dallas is hoping to keep that information from the public."

"Don't worry. I don't intend to ever talk about this again to anyone," she replied. "I don't even want to think about it. Still, that poor woman."

By that time, they had reached her house. He parked in the driveway and together they got out of the truck. He threw his arm around her shoulder as they walked to her front door. Once again, she welcomed his body heat warming her.

"Are you going to be all right here all alone?" he asked when they reached her porch.

She unlocked her door and then turned to face

him. She released a deep, weary sigh. "Yes, I'll be fine." She'd been fine all alone when her husband had walked out on her and she'd been fine when she had lost her parents. She would be okay alone because she had to be.

"If you aren't fine, you have my phone number. Call me, Harper, if you need anything…anything at all," he emphasized. His gaze was so warm, so caring and she wanted to lean forward and feel his arms encircle her once again. But she didn't.

"Thank you, Sam…for everything. I don't know what I would have done without you there with me tonight."

"I'm glad you weren't alone to walk out there and find her like that, and I was glad I could be there for you," he replied.

For just a moment she thought he was going to kiss her. He leaned slightly forward and she saw a flash of something dark and strangely delicious in his eyes.

"Good night, Sam," she said before anything crazy could happen. It had already been a crazy and absolutely awful night. Of course, there was no way she thought a kiss from Sam would be awful. But it also wouldn't be right.

He straightened. "Good night, Harper."

"Thanks for bringing me home," she replied.

"It was no problem."

She stepped into her house and closed and

locked the door behind her. She leaned against the door for several long minutes.

She wondered what her dreams would be tonight. Would she dream of horrifying human scarecrows or would she dream about being held in Sam's arms with his mouth plying hers with heat?

She desperately hoped it was Sam that filled her dreams and not terrifying nightmares of murder.

By the next morning word about the latest murder was out. The headline on the front page of the *Millsville News* read "Scarecrow Killer Strikes Again." To Sam's dismay the story not only named the previous victim and the new one, but also named the bakery as the scene of the crime, which probably meant a lot of people would stop in to ask Harper questions today.

Aside from her initial screams and tears, she had been so strong last night. Despite her fear and her horror, she'd pulled herself together in a remarkably short amount of time. He admired the core of strength she obviously possessed.

Now driving to the bakery, he couldn't help but think about how she had fit so neatly in his arms. It was as if she'd been specifically made for his embrace.

He'd almost kissed her the night before. He'd desperately wanted to pull her back into his arms and take her lips with his. There was no question he was developing a very serious crush on his boss.

He glanced over to the cooler that set in the passenger seat. If she wouldn't go out to dinner with him at the café, then he would bring dinner to her at the bakery.

Today, he was bringing her one of his mother's specialties and he hoped she would take a few minutes and eat it with him after the bakery closed for the day. He hoped it would help take her mind off what had happened the day before, even if just for a few minutes.

He was taking a big chance. She'd already rejected the idea of him taking her out for a date. She might tell him to take the meal and get out. But it was worth taking the chance that she might actually appreciate his effort.

Of course, he wanted to take her out on a real date where they could sit and be waited on and have plenty of time to really get to know each other better, but she seemed to think he was just joking about wanting to take her out. And he wasn't sure how to make her realize he was serious about it... serious about her.

This morning it was certainly much easier thinking about Harper than the horror he had seen the night before. The vision of Sandy was going to be lodged in his mind for a very long time. He could only imagine how Harper was coping today.

Dallas must be pulling his hair out over this latest murder. One had been appalling enough, but two deaths with the women tethered to poles like scarecrows indicated an active killer who probably wasn't done yet.

Who had committed these heinous murders? Certainly, that would be a question on everyone's mind today and for the foreseeable time to come until Dallas had somebody under arrest. He just couldn't imagine anyone in the small town being capable of something like that. But somebody was living with dark secrets and a thirst for murder. He hated that this was happening in his town. He hated that it was happening at all.

He pulled up in front of the bakery and frowned as he saw four other cars already parked in front. So, it had already begun…the lookie-loos would want to see the backyard and others were probably quizzing Harper for any information they could glean from her.

There were also three police cars pulled up along the side of the building, letting Sam know there were officers out there still processing the scene.

Thankfully the backyard was fully fenced with not only a tall privacy fence but also with tall conifer trees that helped add to the seclusion. But it wouldn't help that it was a Saturday when most people were off work and would be able to come to the "scene of the crime."

Although the bakery wasn't really the scene of

the crime. Sandy had been killed someplace else and only staged to be found at the bakery. The newspaper that morning had definitely gotten that fact wrong.

He parked and got out of his truck. Usually, he got right to work outside, but today he beelined inside. There were five people seated at tables and talking to Harper, who wore a slight furrow of uneasiness...of anxiety across her forehead. When he walked in, she smiled at him in what appeared to be immense relief.

"Good morning, Sam," she said.

"'Morning, Harper. I thought I'd start my day off with a cup of coffee and one of your big cinnamon rolls," he said.

"We were just asking Harper about what happened here last night," Joe said.

"You were here last night, Sam. What did you see?" Letta Lee asked. The older woman had never deigned to talk to Sam before. She'd always turned up her nose when Sam was around.

She sat with one of her garden club buddies, another older woman named Mabel Tredway. Mabel had always acted like speaking to the carpenter might dent her standing as one of the "society" women in the small town. Fancy that, they both were willing to talk to him this morning.

"Actually, Harper and I have been firmly instructed not to talk about anything that happened here last night," he replied.

"I've been trying to tell them that," Harper said with a touch of frustration in her tone.

"Oh, surely you can give us a little tidbit of information that wasn't in the paper this morning," Mabel wheedled with a smile. "I heard the birds had pecked out her eyes." She gave a visible shudder. "At least tell us if that is true?"

"Sorry, Mabel. I can't answer that. The last thing Harper and I want to do is tangle with Dallas," he replied firmly. "He told us not to talk about any of it and both Harper and I intend to respect his wishes."

By that time Harper had his coffee and cinnamon roll ready. He paid and then sat at a table. Letta and Mabel left soon after, but several more people drifted in to take their places.

Again, the questions started and Sam repeated what he had told Letta and Mabel. He made the decision then to sit inside for the remainder of the day. Easing Harper's stress today seemed far more important than hammering in a couple of boards.

As the day wore on, Sam changed from coffee and a roll to iced tea and cookies. People continued to drift in and out. The good news was Harper was probably selling more in this single day than she ever had.

The bad news was the customers were all seeking information about the murder that had occurred. He didn't blame them for their curiosity, much of which he believed was driven by fear.

Nothing like this had ever happened in Millsville before. Before Cindy Perry had been killed, Sam couldn't even remember the last time the town had seen a murder.

People would be wondering who they could trust…who might secretly be the killer. Neighbors would be looking askance at each other and family members would be thinking about that odd one in the household.

Sam continued to intercede for Harper by repeating the same thing over and over again to people all day long. He and Harper were not allowed to talk about the crime. Dallas had told them not to discuss anything.

At a few minutes before five, Sam went out to his truck and grabbed the cooler and carried it inside the bakery. He returned to his table and set the cooler at his feet.

Hopefully she would agree to share the meal with him, and hopefully it would erase the lines of stress that had stretched across her forehead throughout the day.

Finally, the last person inside aside from Sam left, and Harper hurried toward the front door where she turned the sign to Closed and then locked up. She turned off the interior lights although there was still plenty of sunshine pouring in through the windows.

She sank down in the chair across from Sam and released a deep sigh. "Jeez. What a long day.

Thank you, Sam, for once again being here for me. I'm sure the last thing you wanted to do was spend your entire day in here fielding questions, but I really appreciate how you ran interference for me."

"At least you sold a lot of cookies today," he said, hoping to see a sparkle return to her eyes.

He achieved his goal. Her eyes not only sparkled, but a small laugh escaped her as well. "There is that," she agreed. "In fact, I sold out of every single one of the cookies I baked this morning. That's never, ever happened before."

"So, it was a good day for cookies but a stressful day for you."

She smiled at him. "Made a bit less stressful thanks to you."

He reached down and picked up the large cooler and placed it in the center of the table. "What's all this?" she asked curiously.

"Since you won't go out to dinner with me, I thought I'd bring a little dinner to you, and I hope you like Italian." Before she could protest, he opened the cooler and brought out the containers that had been packed inside.

"You're in for a real treat. I've got some of my mom's homemade lasagna and meatballs. There's also garlic bread and a bottle of red wine. If you just sit tight, I'll take all these things back to the kitchen and warm them up." He knew she had a microwave in the kitchen.

"Sam…" There was a weak protest in his name. "Why did you go to all this trouble?"

"Because I think you're worth it," he replied easily. He got up from the table and walked behind the display case where he knew she kept plastic cups. He grabbed two and then went back to the table, where he cracked open the bottle of wine and poured two cups.

He set the cooler back on the floor and grabbed the food item containers. "I'll be right back with the meal."

She merely nodded. He was encouraged by her allowing him to do this for her. Once in the kitchen he used the microwave to heat the lasagna and meatballs and threw the garlic bread under the broiler. A few minutes later he plated the food and then carried the two plates back to where she remained seated, sipping her wine.

When he placed her plate before her, she looked up at him with eyes that appeared slightly misty with tears. "Sam, I can't believe you went to all this trouble."

He grinned at her. "If Mohammad won't come to the mountain, then the mountain will come to Mohammad. Now, enjoy."

"Oh, my gosh, this is absolutely amazing," she said after taking her first bite.

"Mom cooks something like this at least once a week and she always sends me home with enough leftovers to feed a small army."

"Do you cook?" She looked at him curiously.

"I do. When I moved out of my parents' home, I quickly realized the only way I was going to get to eat was if I learned how to cook."

"Are you any good at it?" she asked.

He laughed. "I don't know how good I am, but I haven't poisoned myself yet." He was rewarded with her laughter. "What about you? Do you cook anything other than sweet treats?"

"Yes, I cook normal dinners," she replied.

"Are you any good at it?" he asked teasingly.

"I haven't poisoned myself yet," she replied, making him laugh in return.

"What's your specialty?"

"Oh, I don't know. I make a pretty mean parmesan cheese–encrusted pork chop," she replied.

"Hmm, that sounds really good."

For the next few minutes, they ate and talked about different kinds of food. From there, the conversation went to favorite movies and television shows. Like him, she enjoyed watching crime dramas and comedies.

The subjects were safe and easy to talk about and yet gave Sam a little glimpse into who she was as a person...as a woman.

This was exactly what he had wanted, some uninterrupted quality time with her. The more he learned about her, the more attracted he was to her. He was pleased to learn that they seemed to have a lot in common despite their very different jobs.

She liked old country tunes, as did he. She enjoyed long evening walks and crime shows that challenged her. She loved living in Millsville and insisted she would never want to live anywhere else. It was exactly the way he felt about their hometown.

Much to his dismay soon the food had all been eaten and the wine was almost gone. "I'll take care of the dishes," she said.

"Nonsense, I'll help." He got up from the table with her and carried his plate to the back where she had a dishwasher. She rinsed and loaded the plates and then they went back into the front where he packed his now-empty containers back into the cooler.

"It always seems like I'm thanking you for something, Sam," she said once everything was cleaned up.

"If you really want to thank me then you'll agree to go out with me," he replied.

She stared at him for a long moment. "Okay."

He looked at her in stunned surprise. "For real?"

"For real."

"So, you're saying you'll go out with me on a date."

She grinned at him. "That's exactly what I'm saying."

"When?" he asked. "How about tomorrow night around six? We'll go to the café for dinner."

"That sounds good to me," she agreed.

"Then it's a date, right?" He wanted to make sure he was hearing her right.

She laughed. "Yes, Sam, it's a date." Together they walked to the bakery's front door.

"Would you like me to drive or walk you home now?"

"No, I'm fine. I've got a few more things to do here before I leave so I'll just see you in the morning." She unlocked the front door. "Good night, Sam, and thank you again for the wonderful meal among other things."

Sam whistled a happy tune as he walked to his truck. He was grateful that the one thing they hadn't talked about was the body in her backyard. He'd hoped to take her mind off the grisly sight and he believed at least for a little while he had done just that.

What made him even happier was that finally, Harper was seeing him as somebody to date. He wasn't sure why she had changed her mind about him, he was just glad it had happened. For the first time in years Sam was excited about a woman. She not only drew him in physically but emotionally as well.

The last time he'd felt that way about a woman he had fallen in love hard and fast. He'd been twenty-four years old and had believed he'd found the perfect woman who he wanted to spend the rest of his life with.

Sharon was funny and smart and pretty and he'd

loved her desperately. Unfortunately, she hadn't felt the same way about him. After six months of dating, she'd broken up with him. He'd been absolutely devastated.

He was finally willing to put his heart on the line once again. He hoped Harper wasn't just humoring him. His cheerful whistle halted as another thought entered his mind.

Maybe Harper was just toying with him so she could boast to her friends that she was dating a much younger guy. Maybe he was nothing more than a trophy boyfriend for her. Perhaps it would be best that Sam hang on to his heart before seeing where this all was going.

Chapter 4

What have you done? Girl, you must have lost your ever-loving mind. What in the world were you thinking? The next evening at five forty-five, Harper stared at her reflection in her bathroom mirror. What on earth had made her agree to go out on a date with the much younger, very hunky Sam Bravano?

Even as the question shot through her head, she knew the answer. She'd agreed to go out with him because he had been so gentle and caring with her on the night Sandy Blackstone had been found. She'd agreed because he had sung her "Happy Birthday" and brought her dinner.

Ultimately, she'd capitulated because he made her laugh and because he'd been so tenacious about wanting to take her out on a date. Besides that, she'd agreed because she genuinely liked him.

"It's just one night," she told the reflection in the mirror. It wasn't like she was going to sleep with him, although the idea was certainly appealing. She'd go out with him this one time and then not again. The whole idea of him wanting any kind of a real romantic relationship with a slightly chubby, menopausal woman who was years older than him was ridiculous.

She turned away from the mirror and left the bathroom.

Her makeup had been applied and she was clad in a lavender sundress that hid her tummy and hips and instead skimmed the length of her body. White earrings and sandals completed her outfit.

She went into the living room and sank down on the sofa to await Sam's arrival. She'd spent the day waffling between phoning him to call the whole thing off or biting the bullet and going. She'd finally decided to bite the bullet. One and done, she told herself firmly. He probably wouldn't want another date with her anyway.

She'd also spent the day doing a little housework and reading a novel by her favorite author. It had been a restful day after a crazy and disturbing week.

The town was all still buzzing about the Scarecrow Killer and his newest victim. The idea of a potential serial killer at work in the small town was frightening, indeed.

Dallas had called for a town meeting in the community hall the next night and she intended to be there. She was sure that most of the people in town, along with all the farmers on the outskirts of town, would also attend.

Still, even with all these things swirling around in her head, it was thoughts of Sam that took precedence. Out of all the women in town, why did he want to spend time with her?

She'd been tossed away by her husband because she hadn't been young enough, hadn't been fun enough. She'd been left behind because she wasn't pretty enough, wasn't witty enough to keep the man who had vowed to love her forever. So, why on earth would she be enough for Sam?

She was getting way ahead of herself. By the end of this evening, she was fairly sure Sam wouldn't be interested in another date with her. She supposed this one date wouldn't hurt anything. All she really wanted from Sam was his expertise as a carpenter. This night was just the result of him catching her at a weak moment.

At precisely six o'clock a knock fell on her door. Her heart did a crazy dance in her chest. She got up, grabbed her purse and then answered. It was Sam…a very hot, handsome Sam. She'd never seen him dressed in anything but jeans and a T-shirt. Tonight, he wore black slacks with a short-sleeved forest green dress shirt that showcased his beautiful green eyes.

"Hi, Harper. You look positively stunning," he said as his gaze swept the length of her.

She felt the blush that warmed her cheeks. "Thanks. I'm all ready to go." Even though she didn't believe him when he said things like that to her, there was no question that it was still nice to hear.

"Are you hungry?" he asked once they were in his truck. He smelled as delicious as he looked with the spicy cologne that she always found so wonderfully attractive.

"I am." A nervous tension fluttered inside her as she thought of going out in public with Sam. The café was always packed on Sunday evenings. There would be a lot of people there who would see the two of them together out on a social basis. What on earth would they think? "What about you?"

"I'm definitely ready for a big juicy burger. Unfortunately, I don't think the café does Mexican food very often."

She was surprised he'd remembered that she'd mentioned in passing that Mexican was her favorite type of food. "They don't, but I always find something good on the menu."

"It's a nice night," he said. "Although still a little warm."

"At least it's cooled off some from this afternoon," she replied.

The closer they got to the café, the more nervous she was becoming. She should have never agreed to this. What were people going to think when they saw the two of them out together?

"Relax, Harper," Sam said as if reading her mood. "It's just a meal out, not a lifetime commitment."

She laughed. "I realize that."

"Have you ever been to the Farmer's Club?" he asked as they passed the place.

The Farmer's Club was a small bar on Main Street mostly frequented by the older farmers and couples in the area. "No, I've never been in there, although I've heard about it from some of the people who come into the bakery."

"It's a nice place that caters to an older crowd versus Murphy's, which is much bigger and noisier and caters to more of the singles in town. Maybe next time we go out we can have a drink and relax at the Farmer's Club."

She didn't feel like this was the appropriate moment to tell him there wouldn't be a next time. "At least you'll be able to get one of your big juicy cheeseburgers for dinner," she said in an attempt to change the subject.

"Yeah, and I'm definitely hungry tonight. On another note, I heard that the long-term weather forecast is for a couple of days of rain this week.

And just so you know, this man doesn't work in the rain," he replied.

"I wouldn't expect you to," she replied. "I guess your work is at the mercy of the weather at times."

"Definitely," he agreed. "Rain can keep me off a job for days, so I'm not particularly fond of rainy days."

"Sundays… I don't mind a rainy Sunday occasionally."

He shot a quick glance at her and smiled. "And what do you like to do on rainy Sundays?"

"Nothing exciting. I enjoy curling up on my sofa under a nice warm blanket and watching movies all day."

"So, you aren't one of those crazy women who like to get naked and dance in the rain?"

"Good grief, no," she replied with a laugh.

By that time, they had arrived at the café. Just as she had feared, cars were parked not only in front of the place but also all the way down the block.

"Looks like we'll have a little walk," he said as he pulled into a parking space across the street and down the block from the eating establishment. He cut the engine and smiled at her. "Sit tight."

He got out of the truck and then walked around to open her door and help her down. She murmured a thank you and then they started walking side by side toward the café.

It seemed only natural when he reached out and took her hand in his. The warm, slightly calloused

hand felt familiar and good and she remembered
how he had held her hand the night that Sandy's
body had been found. But she didn't want to think
about that right now.

"It looks like there's a big crowd here tonight,"
she said.

"Yeah. Hopefully we'll be able to grab a booth
or a table without waiting too long," he replied.

He dropped her hand as they reached the café
door and he ushered her inside. A cacophony of
sound greeted them, the clinking of silverware and
dishes and people talking and laughing together.

Along with the sounds were the heavenly scents.
They were the fragrances of cooking meats and
onions, of simmering stews and veggies. Finally,
there was a hint of yeasty rolls and fresh-baked
pies.

The decor in the café was an homage to the
local farmers. One wall held big golden hay bales
with bright red roosters. Another wall depicted
a yellow cornfield with the three tall silos that
were part of the town's skyscape, and yet another
was farmland in patterns of browns and greens
and golds.

Harper had always found the café to be a pleasant, calming place to eat. But tonight, as Sam spied
an empty booth in the back and as they made their
way toward it, she was aware of gazes following
them and conversations suddenly turning to whis-
pers. She also caught a quick glance of her friend

Allie Crawford and her husband, Ed, seated at one of the tables they passed.

She had no idea who else might be in the café that she knew for she tried to keep her gaze straight ahead, not making eye contact with anyone. She didn't want to see the expressions on their faces, although she definitely felt the stares.

She was grateful to slide into the booth where at least she couldn't see everyone who had been staring at them. She immediately grabbed one of the menus that stood between the salt and pepper shakers and held it up in front of her face.

"Harper." Sam's deep voice made her lower the menu and look at him over the top edge. "Relax. I promise you, it's going to be just fine."

She released a small, nervous laugh and lowered the menu all the way. "I felt like everyone in the whole café was gawking at us and whispering about us. I'm sure they're wondering what you are doing here with such an old lady."

He frowned at her. "Harper, you have got to stop thinking of yourself that way. You are not an old lady. You are a beautiful and vibrant woman and to be perfectly honest, I don't care what other people think. I'm here with the woman I want to be here with. Now, smile and at least try to look like you're enjoying my company." He grinned, causing his dimple to dance in his cheek.

She laughed again. "Okay, I'm relaxing as you speak."

"Good, now let's take a minute and decide what we want to eat."

She returned her gaze to the menu, but her thoughts remained on Sam. There was no question he made her feel good. He made her feel pretty and girly. She couldn't remember the last time a man had told her she was beautiful. Did she believe his words? Not really, but she definitely enjoyed hearing them. In any case, after tonight they would go back to being only employer and employee.

Regina Waltz, a pleasant young blonde, appeared at the side of their booth to take their orders. "Hey, Sam… Harper, what can I get for you two this evening?"

"I'd like the turkey bacon club with fries on the side," she said.

"And I'll have the big bacon cheeseburger with a side of fries," Sam said. They both ordered iced tea and Regina left to put their orders in.

He put their menus back in place and then settled back in the booth and smiled at her. "So, how was your day off today?"

"Nice and quiet. I did a little housework and then read for a while. It's too hot to do much of anything outside, although I certainly don't have to tell that to you. What about you? How was your day?"

"Fairly productive. I finished ripping out the ugliest lime green and yellow linoleum you'd ever want to see out of my kitchen."

"What are you putting down instead?"

"I haven't quite decided yet. It's either going to be some nice, big neutral ceramic tiles or some sort of a wood product. Maybe you could come over to my place one evening and give me a woman's perspective on it."

His gaze on her was so warm, so inviting. Yet, she was also aware of the couple at the table nearest to them shooting her disapproving glares. "We'll see," she finally replied.

For the next few minutes, they small-talked about the weather and then the town meeting the next night. By that time their dinners had arrived.

Even though she tried to completely relax, there was still a core of anxiety inside her. How much gossip was now flying around with her and Sam as the main subjects? She was far too old for Sam and most of the people in town probably thought she was an extremely foolish woman.

It didn't help that Sam was so danged hot…that he could probably date any young beautiful woman the town had to offer. And everyone knew that. If people weren't outraged by the idea of their May-December date, then they were probably pitying Harper for being stupid enough to believe there could ever be something between her and Sam.

And what were they saying about Sam? They probably couldn't imagine what was in his head to want to be with Harper. And as she gazed into Sam's beautiful green eyes, she knew the foolishness had to stop tonight. Even if he didn't want it to stop, she would put an end to it.

Because she liked him…she liked him far more than she should.

Sam had been aware of the curious gazes that had followed them as they had walked to their booth. He could also feel Harper's discomfort and he truly hated that for her.

She definitely didn't see herself as Sam saw her. He found her beautiful and with a wonderful sense of humor. She was strong and a successful businesswoman. He didn't feel any age difference when he was with her, when he was talking and laughing with her. For him, she was the complete package and he couldn't believe she hadn't been snapped up by a man long before now.

"Do you date a lot?" he now asked, eager to learn as much as he could about her.

She paused with a French fry halfway between her plate and her mouth. "Oh yes, I have a date every couple of decades or so," she replied dryly.

He looked at her in genuine surprise. "I'm shocked that your social calendar isn't full with dates every weekend. What's wrong with all the men in this town?"

She laughed. "I've asked myself that several times in the past few years."

Oh, he loved the musical sound of her laughter,

and the way her mirth not only filled the air but also caused her eyes to sparkle so brightly.

"You were married for a long time, right?"

"Almost nineteen years," she replied.

"What happened to cause a divorce?" He immediately winced. "Or maybe I'm getting way too personal. If so, I'm sorry and please just ignore the question."

"No, it's okay. What happened to cause my divorce? Her name was Ginger and she was a twenty-five-year-old with big breasts and a desire to marry my husband. According to my husband, she was everything I wasn't…fun and lively and gorgeous among other things. I'm not sure how long he was cheating on me with her, but ultimately, he told me his happiness was with her and so he was leaving me." She released a small sigh. "That afternoon he packed up his bags and left and that was pretty much that."

Even though the words were said matter-of-factly, he saw the flash of pain that momentarily filled her eyes. So, she'd been replaced by a much younger model, and after nineteen years of marriage that had to have been a big blow to her very soul.

"I'm so sorry that happened to you," he said. "He was obviously a jerk who only had half a brain. He apparently didn't know how to appreciate the finer things in life."

She laughed. "I like the way you think, Sam."

"Well, it's true. Do you ever miss him?"

"My husband? No, not at all. He obviously wasn't the stand-up man I thought he was. But there are definitely times I miss having somebody to talk to…to share with." She shrugged her shoulders. "Still, if I'm meant to be alone, then I'm just fine with that. I don't mind my own company and I'm comfortable in my own skin. I have my work and for the most part that fulfills me."

That was one of the many things that drew him to her: the fact that she knew who she was and she was fine with it. He liked her sense of self-confidence. He found it sexy as well.

They were quiet and concentrated on eating for the next few minutes. "What about you?" she finally asked, breaking the silence that had been between them.

"What about me?" he asked.

"Do you have a sob story about a love in your past?"

"Certainly nothing like what you experienced with your marriage. I was twenty-four years old when I fell in love for the first and only time. She was everything I thought I wanted for the rest of my life and for six months I thought it all went wonderfully well. But before long I realized there was trouble in paradise."

He paused to take a drink and then continued.

"I guess I was so crazy about her, I hadn't seen or really paid attention to all the red flags."

"Like what?" Harper asked. He was glad to see that she was no longer looking around at the other diners but rather completely absorbed in their conversation.

"She mentioned several times to me that she didn't really like small-town living. She also hinted around that she wanted me to find a different job, something more impressive than a mere carpenter. But I pretty much ignored those things and then was completely blindsided when she broke up with me and ended up moving to Kansas City to be with a man who was a lawyer she had met on the internet."

"I'm so sorry that happened to you," she replied. "Broken hearts always hurt, whether you've been married for years or are together for a shorter amount of time."

"At least my heartbreak was a long time ago," he replied. "Did you miss some red flags with your husband?"

She laughed again. "Oh my gosh, I missed a whole parade of red flags. In the last year of our marriage, he was suddenly working late most evenings when he had never had to work late before. There were many times he didn't answer his phone when I'd call. He had one dumb excuse after another, for not answering the phone or not being where he'd told me he would be, yet I always believed him. Despite all those things, I never suspected for one minute that he was having an affair until the day he left me."

She picked up a French fry and dragged it through a pool of ketchup on her plate. When she looked up at him her eyes were clear and bright with no shadows or pain to cloud them. "You like to think the people you trust have the same integrity and morals as you, but I guess it doesn't always happen that way."

"That's why it's so important that two people have open communication and conversations about such things. Personally, I've always believed in ending a relationship before starting a new one and I consider myself a monogamous man who would never cheat if I was married."

She smiled at him. It was a real, open smile that lit up her entire face and created a pool of heat that swirled around deep in his stomach. "It's time to lighten up this discussion. Why don't you tell me more about your family?"

For the next half an hour or so he regaled her with stories from his childhood, making her laugh over and over again. He loved making her laugh and he had plenty of funny stories about life with the Bravano family.

"I always wanted a sibling, and your stories about life with your brothers make me feel like I definitely lost out."

"Were you lonely as an only child?" he asked.

"Not always, but there were certainly times

when I was. My mom and dad tried their best to make sure I wouldn't feel that way but their efforts didn't always succeed. According to my mother, they hadn't intended for me to be an only child and they tried to give me a sibling, but it just never happened."

By that time their meals were done, but he wasn't ready to call it a night. He wasn't ready to take her home and tell her good-night yet. "I'm thinking maybe a piece of apple pie and a cup of coffee would be good right about now," he said. "What would you like for dessert?"

"I would usually say nothing, but if you really force me to have dessert, then apple pie and coffee sounds good," she replied. He was glad she didn't indicate that she was immediately ready to go home.

He grinned. "You have total permission to blame me for you ordering and enjoying dessert." He motioned to Regina and ordered their pie and coffee.

Minutes later they were enjoying their apple pie and talking about other favorite desserts. "Of course, my favorite is cake," she said.

"I wouldn't expect you to say anything else," he replied with a grin. "And I would assume your favorite cake is the kind you baked for your birthday."

"You would guess right," she replied.

"I have to admit, I'm now a total fan of your cookies."

She smiled. "I've noticed."

She then began to entertain him with bakery horror stories, from accidentally using the wrong ingredients to giving the wrong cake to the wrong people.

"I once baked a cake that was to be served after an older man's funeral and at the same time I had a birthday cake for a six-year-old girl going out," she began.

"Oh no, don't tell me," he said with a laugh.

"I'm telling you. I'm not sure who was more horrified, the people after the funeral who got the pink-and-yellow-flowered birthday cake or the little girl when her mother opened the cake box to discover a black cake that read 'We'll miss you, Grandpa.' But I definitely heard from both unhappy parties."

She was a lively storyteller. Her eyes sparkled and all her features lit up. Was that the way she would look when making love with him? The thought jumped into his brain unexpectedly. But once it was there it refused to dislodge easily.

He was definitely physically attracted to her and would take her to bed in a fast minute, but he knew he couldn't rush things with her. He didn't want just a quick hookup. He wanted something more meaningful than that. He needed to woo her a little longer. Besides, he had a feeling she was well worth the wait.

Finally, it was time to go. Their dessert plates were empty and their coffee was gone. He waved to Regina to get his check and after paying they got up to leave.

Immediately he felt the tension fill Harper once again and he knew it was because they had to walk through the café to get back to the front door.

She walked stiffly beside him, her gaze directed straight at the door. He hated that she was so self-conscious about being seen with him when he was so proud to be seen with her.

The tension appeared to leave her the moment they stepped back outside. Once again, he reached for her hand. He loved the way hers felt enclosed in his. Her hand was small and dainty and her skin was so soft and warm.

"I am so full," she announced once they were back in his truck and headed to her house.

"That makes two of us," he replied.

"I probably should have said no to dessert."

"Ah, but never regret the dessert you eat. Instead regret the dessert you don't eat," he said.

She grinned at him. "Did some wise old man tell you that?"

He laughed. "I don't remember, but it might have been my mother."

"Ah, a wise woman," she replied.

Night had fallen and she looked enchanting in

the soft illumination from the dashboard. Once again, a wave of intense physical attraction toward her punched him in the gut.

"So, it's back to work tomorrow," he said, breaking the silence that had momentarily grown between them.

"Yes, it's back to cakes and cupcakes and everything sweet for me," she replied. "At least I feel well rested to start a new week."

"That's good. I'm ready to get back to work, too." By that time, he had reached her house. He pulled into her driveway, shut off the engine and then hurried around to the passenger door to help her out.

When they reached her front porch, she unlocked her door and then turned back to face him. "Thank you, Sam. I really had a lovely evening tonight."

"I really enjoyed it, too." He took a step closer to her, so close he could feel her body heat wafting toward him and smell the seductive scent of her. "Harper, can I kiss you good-night?"

Her eyes flared wide, but to his encouragement, she didn't step back from him. "I... Uh...okay, I guess."

Before she could change her mind, he gathered her into his arms and took her mouth with his. Oh, she tasted so hot and sweet, with just a hint of the apple and cinnamon from the pie she'd just eaten. When she opened her mouth to him, he quickly deepened the kiss, swirling his tongue with hers.

Oh, the woman definitely knew how to kiss. Her lips were pillowy soft and he felt himself quickly getting aroused. The kiss lasted only a few moments and then, with a small gasp, she halted it and stepped back from him. "Thank you again, Sam. Good night."

"Good night, Harper."

She went into her house and he turned and headed to his truck.

It had been a really great night. Hopefully the ice had been broken with the date tonight. And hopefully she would want to go out with him again.

Everything he learned about her only drew him closer to her. He wanted to discover so much more about her. He wanted to know what she thought about a hundred…a thousand things. He wished to learn all her likes and dislikes and all of her hopes and dreams.

He only hoped she felt the same way about him. He knew the age thing bothered her, but he was hoping with more time she would see her way past that. The difference in their ages certainly didn't bother him at all.

He didn't know where things were going with her. All he could hope for at this point was that she wanted to go out with him again.

He leaned forward in his chair, the *Millsville News* in front of him. He was back in the news, headline status. The Scarecrow Killer had returned with a vengeance and he knew the whole town was afraid. There was even a town meeting planned that would be solely about him.

The very thought made excitement roar through him and his entire body positively tingled with intense pleasure. Nobody in this town had ever really seen him before, but they were definitely seeing him now. He knew the young women of Millsville were going to bed every night with fear in their hearts. Some of them were probably having nightmares. All because of him.

He loved it. He loved all of it. He loved sedating them and dragging them into his car. He loved the warmth of their blood when he stabbed them and their pleas and cries before that, while they bargained for their lives.

He liked slowly stripping them naked and then redressing them in their special scarecrow attire. Once they had been dead for a couple of hours, he then sewed their lips together.

He saved the best thing for last. The eyes. The windows to the soul. The very last thing he did was take out their eyes…blue eyes like his mother's, God rest her soul.

He now looked over to the wooden shelving where two jars sat side by side. One held Cindy's eyeballs and the other held Sandy's. Unfortunately, they hadn't kept their bright blue color but instead had turned a milky faint bluish white.

Even though that had initially disappointed him,

he now realized maybe it was better that way, for if he sat and stared at the blue eyes that so reminded him of his mother, he would not only be filled with a rich rage, but also with the trembling fear she'd always evoked in him.

That bitch. She had terrorized him until five years ago when she'd "accidentally" fallen down the basement stairs and broken her neck. To the outside world she'd been admired as a strong woman who was a single parent. But to him… she'd been the very devil.

There was no fear inside him today, only a sweet, heady jubilation. He pushed the papers aside, leaned back in his chair and instead looked around him. This was actually the basement of the small ranch house his mother had left to him upon her tragic death, but he thought of this space as his killing lair. After all, his first murder had been that of his mother, who had died at the bottom of the stairs.

The shelving not only held the two jars of eyeballs, but also the items he would need for future kills. There were straw hats and flannel shirts, jeans in a variety of sizes, along with his killing knife and the instruments necessary to sew together lips and remove eyeballs.

There was also a stack of thick, sturdy poles, perfect for binding a woman to in order to make her an impeccable scarecrow. And he had plenty of poles…plenty of all the supplies he needed to keep him in the headlines. Plenty to keep the young women of Millsville terrified for a very long time to come.

Looking at it all now, the hunger inside him rose up…the intense hunger to make another scarecrow. But he'd practice self-control. He'd wait. He'd attend the town meeting tomorrow night and he'd act like another concerned citizen. It would be such fun to feel the terror of the entire town as they all came together to talk about him.

After that, he'd go hunting again and when he found the perfect woman, he'd turn her into a perfect scarecrow. Maybe this one would finally stop the screaming in his head.

Chapter 5

The next evening, the community center was packed with people. Dallas was supposed to begin talking at seven. At six forty-five Harper entered the large room where chairs were set up before the stage, upon which stood a podium.

A gathering like this was always a big deal. The café had set up coffee and brought doughnuts for everyone and Harper had packaged up dozens of cookies and cupcakes to give away for the event.

The last time she remembered there being a big town meeting like this was four years ago when spring storms had torn through the area, leaving some of the farmers with damage to their homes and outbuildings.

At that time the meeting had been about supporting those neighbors in their time of need. Garage and bake sales were set up with all the proceeds going to the people who needed extra help in just getting the basics. Volunteer task forces were also set up to provide physical aid in rebuilding and repairing.

The room now buzzed with dozens of conversations as neighbors greeted neighbors. The talk wasn't just about the recent murder, but also about weather and crops and kids and other current events. Many in the farming community didn't come into town very often, so this was a good opportunity for them to catch up with other people.

It appeared that everyone in the whole town had shown up. Still, despite the crowd, as she made her way to one of the empty chairs, Sam appeared at her side.

She had spent the entire day once again distracted by him as he'd worked outside of her shop. Just after noon he'd come inside for his cookie lunch break and since it was just the two of them inside at that moment, she had sat with him.

As always, the conversation had been a combination of him lightheartedly flirting with her and her laughing in response. Before Sam, she hadn't laughed very much. Before him, she hadn't felt pretty and worth flirting with.

"Hey, stranger," he now said to her with the brilliant smile that always warmed her deep inside.

"Hi, Sam," she replied. He had offered to bring

her tonight but she had declined his offer. Still, every time she saw him, every time he flirted with her and she remembered what fun it had been to be out with him, her resolve to never go out with him again weakened more than a little bit.

"Mind if I sit with you?" he asked.

"Not at all," she replied.

They found two empty chairs toward the back of the room and once again she felt some of the disapproving looks that followed them. Jeez, surely these people had something other than who the baker was sitting with to worry about in their lives. They were here about a couple of horrid murders, for crying out loud.

"You're going to have to get used to it," Sam leaned over and whispered to her. "Because I don't intend to let a bunch of small-minded people deter me from seeing you."

So, he noticed the glares, too. It warmed her that apparently she was the woman he wanted to be with…at least for now. Should she not see him anymore because other people disapproved? Should she deprive herself of his company even though she enjoyed him a lot? This whole situation with Sam confused her.

Even now, with the crowd surrounding them, the scent of him enticed her. His nearness excited her. The kiss they had shared after their date had been more than wonderful. So, should she stop dating him because some people might want to criticize her for it?

Before she could answer any of her own questions, a hush fell over the crowd as Dallas took his place at the podium. He looked quite handsome in his uniform, but he also appeared tired and grim.

"As you all have probably heard by now, Sandy Blackstone lost her life several days ago. She was killed by the same man who we believe murdered Cindy Perry," he began.

He then went on to speak about how the victims were found, dispelling any rumors and gossip that had swirled around. However, the one thing he didn't mention was that Sandy's eyes had been removed. Harper had heard through the grapevine that Cindy's eyes had been missing as well, but Dallas didn't mention anything about her eyes, either.

"There is still a lot about these crimes that we don't know. Obviously, we don't know who the killer is. We also don't know where these women were killed before they were staged to be found first in a cornfield and then behind the bakery," Dallas continued.

"We don't know why this person is killing or why the bodies are being left where they are. So, I'm calling on you all to keep your eyes and ears open and come to me with any information you might have. So far, both of the victims have had blond hair and blue eyes, but we're not sure this will be a pattern that continues. Therefore, I'm telling all women to travel in twos or a group whenever you're out and about. Be aware of your surroundings and who you let into your personal space."

His words were sobering and shot a chill up Harper's spine. Basically, he was telling them that any woman could be the next victim. Any women in Millsville could become the next horrific scare-crow.

At the end of his speech, Dallas took no questions. He left the stage and immediately disappeared. Sam turned toward her. "I think I'm going to go grab a couple of cookies and a cup of coffee. Would you like for me to get you something?"

"No, thanks. I'm good."

"Will you sit and wait for me to get back?" he asked.

"Okay," she agreed.

He had only been gone a minute or two when Harper's friends Becky and Allie appeared in his place. "Hey, girls, what's happening?" she said in greeting.

"I think what's important is that you tell us what's happening with you," Allie replied with one of her dark eyebrows raised.

"What do you mean?" Harper asked in confusion. "There's nothing really going on with me."

"Apparently there is. Allie told me you and Sam went out to dinner together," Becky said as she sat in the chair Sam had vacated. "Please tell me it was a strictly business dinner."

"Actually, it was a date...a strictly for pleasure dinner date," Harper replied.

"My God, Harper, what on earth are you thinking? Have you completely lost your mind?" Allie asked. "You know he's probably just toying with you. He can't be seriously attracted to you."

"Gee, thanks," Harper replied dryly.

"You know what I mean," Allie replied. "Harper, you know I think you're a real catch, but not for a man who is so much younger than you."

"What does he really want from you?" Becky asked.

"Nothing. Nothing but my company," Harper replied defensively.

"Honestly, Harper. I just thought you had more sense than this. Surely you can't believe this would work out," Becky said with a disapproving shake of her head.

"Who says I want anything to work out with him?" Harper finally got a little bit hot under the collar. "Maybe I'm just having a bit of fun with Sam. What's wrong with that?" She looked at each of her friends with a touch of defiance.

"There's just been some talk. People don't like it. They don't think it's right," Becky said.

"So, I should stop having fun with Sam because some people in this town don't think it's right? Maybe they're all just jealous."

"Oh, Harper," Becky said with dismay.

"I don't think that's the case," Allie protested.

"Well, no matter what the case is, I'm not going to let anyone make my decision about whether I see Sam on a social basis or not. I'll decide that for myself." Harper sat up straighter in her chair. "But thank you both for thinking about my happiness."

"Harper, the very last thing we want to do is make you mad or upset. We just want to protect you. You just have to wonder what a hot-looking young man like Sam is doing with you." Allie took Harper's hand. "Still friends?"

"Of course," Harper replied. But she was definitely irritated with the two of them. Who did they think they were to tell her what to do with her life? Who to see or not see in her spare time? It wasn't as if the two of them were jumping to spend any real time with her. Heck, they'd both even missed her little birthday party.

And why were they so certain that Sam couldn't really be attracted to her? That he couldn't truly enjoy her company without wanting anything from her? That really hurt her feelings and reminded her of the negative way she had felt about herself when her husband had left her.

They finally left Harper's side and Tom Adamson stopped by her chair. Tom was one of her morning regulars and greeted her with a friendly smile. "How are you doing this evening, Harper?"

"I'm doing fine. How are you doing?" she asked.

"Okay. Troubling meeting, right?"

She nodded. "It was definitely troubling," she agreed.

"Well, I'm heading out now. I'll see you at the bakery tomorrow," he said.

"See you, Tom."

The older man murmured a good-night and then wove his way to the end of the aisle.

Sam returned with his coffee and cookies. He sank back down next to her and smiled. "Thanks for waiting for me. I hate to eat cookies all alone."

She laughed and for the next couple of moments he munched on a cookie and drank his coffee. "At least the crowd is starting to thin out a bit. By the time you finish your coffee and cookies we should have no problem getting out of here," she said.

"Yeah, that's why I figured I'd wait until the initial mad dash for the exit was over before trying to leave," he replied.

"Is your family here?" she asked curiously.

"My mother didn't come but my two brothers were here earlier however they've already left," he replied. "I saw you visiting with a couple of your friends."

She frowned. "We weren't really visiting. They were basically telling me I was a fool and needed to stop seeing you." She looked down at her lap. "They couldn't believe that you would really be interested in me and they're sure I'm going to get hurt. They implied that I look like a foolish old lady with you and that people disapprove of us together."

"Harper, look at me." She looked up and into his beautiful eyes. "If I were you, I'd get really tired and more than a little bit angry at people implying that you somehow aren't enough to hold my attention. If it's a matter of them thinking I'm somehow using you, then what am I using you for? For your money? I don't need your money, I have plenty of my own. Do they think I'm using you for a quick hookup? To be perfectly honest I could get a hookup every single night of the week, but that's not what I'm looking for."

"Then what are you looking for with me?" she asked.

"Aside from the fact that I think you're beautiful both inside and out, I find you intelligent and I enjoy having conversations with you. You have a wonderful sense of humor and I like laughing with you. I like that you're a strong woman who is confident in your own skin."

He paused a moment and then continued, "Harper, I'm just into you and some things don't need to or can't be explained. It's a matter of chemistry. Now, are you going to allow other people to dictate who you should or shouldn't date?"

He reached out and took her hand in his. "Harper, right now we're a novelty item to gossip about. People would rather gossip about us than think about the two murders that have occurred,

murders that have everyone frightened. But tomorrow or the day after everyone will find something else to gossip about. I promise you this will
pass and eventually nobody will care what we're
doing together. Now, I'd like to ask you out again.
Are you in?"

She held his gaze while a million emotions and
thoughts flew around in her head. She had been
so sure she wasn't going to go out with him again.
One and done, that was what she'd believed where
dating him was concerned.

However, ultimately it came down to one important thing: What did she really want for herself? And in this moment, she decided she wanted
Sam.

"I'm in," she answered.

He smiled and squeezed her hand. "That's my
girl. How about tomorrow night I take you to the
Farmer's Club for drinks and some good conversation?"

"That sounds nice," she replied. To heck with
everyone else and what they thought. She was
willing to see where this thing with Sam went. It
wasn't as if her heart was involved. She was just
enjoying his company. Right now, she was just
having fun with him.

As he finished up his last cookie, she looked
around the room and realized there was almost
no one else left inside. The coffee machine had
been packed away, the doughnuts and cookies had

disappeared and three men were folding up the chairs and carrying them to the storage closet next to the stage.

"We need to get out of here, otherwise we're going to be folded up and shoved in the closet," she observed.

"That would not be a good thing," he said with a laugh and together they rose. "I'm going to follow you home," he said as they exited the building.

"Why? That really isn't necessary."

"I think it's necessary and it's because it's after dark and you're all alone and your safety matters to me," he replied.

"Oh...okay, thanks." It had been a very long time since anyone had cared if she got home safely from someplace or not. After all the warnings they had just gotten from Dallas, she wasn't going to turn down his offer.

He saw her to her car and then hurried across the parking lot to get into his truck. She waited until his truck was right behind her to pull out of the parking lot.

She had another date with Sam and she was probably going to catch more hell from her friends. But she didn't care. She'd been alone for a very long time now and it felt good to have somebody to share things with,...somebody to talk to and laugh with. She was doing this for herself and not to please anyone else and, aside from her work, it had been a long time since she'd done something to make herself happy.

When she reached her house, she parked in the driveway and got out of her car. She waved to Sam and then hurried toward her front door, thankful that she'd left her porch light on.

She saw it immediately and her heart began to thunder loudly in her ears as the back of her throat closed up in stunned shock.

"It" appeared to be an old woman fashion doll hanging on a wreath holder she had on her front door. A nail file was pushed through the doll's head and a note was folded and tucked beneath one of her arms.

Who had done this? Who had left this horrible thing on her front door? She stumbled several steps backward. She spun around toward where Sam's truck was still parked at the curb. He opened his door. "Harper, is everything okay?" he yelled to her.

"N-no, it's not." That was all she could manage to say as her throat continued to squeeze closed with shock.

And that was all she needed to say for Sam to jump out of the truck and came running to her side. He immediately saw the doll and ripped it off the wreath holder. "Let's go inside," he said tersely.

With trembling fingers, she unlocked the door, opened it and then flew into her living room. Sam followed her in and shut and locked the door behind him.

She walked with shaky legs to the sofa and sank down. He joined her there, plucking the note from under the doll's arm and then placing the doll on the coffee table in front of them.

A deep frown cut across his forehead as he opened the note. "What does it say?" she asked, consciously trying to keep her gaze away from the horrible, mutilated doll.

"'Have you lost your brain?'" he read. "'Date somebody your own age.'" He tossed the note on the coffee table. "This really pisses me off." He got up from the sofa and pulled his cell phone from his back pocket. "I need to call Dallas. Maybe he can catch the bastard who left this for you."

She nodded and fought against an icy chill that threatened to crawl up her back. Who had done this? Who had left this atrocity on her door? Who cared so much about who she was dating? Obviously, it had to have been somebody who saw them together tonight at the town meeting and had left the community center before them. That was almost the entire town.

She was vaguely aware of Sam making the call to Dallas and then he returned to sit next to her. He took her hands in his and she welcomed the familiar warmth of his touch against her icy fingers.

"Honey, don't be afraid," he said softly. "This

was done by a coward…a jerk who wants to try to bully you. I hope you don't let this get to you."

"I just can't imagine who would do such a horrible thing. Who would care enough about my dating habits to go to all this trouble?" She searched his handsome features as if she might find the answers there.

"Hopefully, Dallas will be able to tell us who did this," he replied.

"Us." It was nice to know she wasn't all alone in this, that Sam was taking this on as his issue, too. "Has anyone else asked you out recently? Maybe somebody who would see me as their competition?" he asked and released his grasp on her hands.

"No," she replied. "Nobody has asked me out for at least a year or so."

A little over a year ago she had gone out on one date with Billy Jackson. He was a nice older man who worked at the post office. They had gone out to dinner together at the café but had quickly realized they had very little in common and there had been absolutely no sparks between them. They hadn't gone on a second date and he had just recently married a nice woman who worked at the grocery store. Since then, nobody else had asked her out. Nobody had shown any kind of a romantic interest in her. Not until Sam.

She and Sam sat in silence for several long minutes. She was still trying to wrap her mind around the horrid doll that had been left for her. Who on earth would even think to do such a thing? Who would think to drive a nail file into a doll's head? It was positively sick.

"Harper." Sam said her name softly. She turned to look at him again. "It's going to be all right. I swear it's just a stupid scare tactic."

"Well, it worked because right now I'm scared," she replied.

"Try not to be," he replied. "I really believe whoever did this isn't a real threat to you."

She desperately wanted to believe him, but she couldn't help the shivers of fear that continued to race up and down her back.

Again, they fell into silence and minutes later a knock sounded at her door. It was Dallas, and she was hoping the lawman would be able to tell her whether she should really be afraid or not.

As Dallas questioned Harper, Sam once again took one of her hands in his to show his support. Her hand felt so small and trembled slightly as she told Dallas she had no idea who would be this angry that she was seeing Sam.

Dammit, he hated that she was so frightened. He hated the dark shadows that had taken over the beautiful sparkle of her blue eyes… the fear that tightened her lush lips into a thin slash. And he hated that this had happened because he was seeing her.

"Two of my girlfriends talked to me tonight after the meeting about not liking the fact that I'd gone out with Sam on a date," she now said.

"Their names?" Dallas asked.

"Becky Barlow and Allie Crawford, but neither of them would stoop so low as to do something like this," Harper said. "They're nice women and they would never, ever even think about doing something as crazy, as awful as that." She gestured to the doll in front of her.

"What about you, Sam?"

Sam straightened up and looked at Dallas in surprise. "What about me?"

"Are there any women out there who might have a problem with you seeing Harper?"

"Not that I'm aware of," Sam replied.

"Any women who have made it clear they'd like to go out with you?" Dallas asked.

Sam was aware of Harper gazing at him curiously. "Uh, Celeste Winthrop has let me know on more than one occasion she'd like me to ask her out, but I've tried to make it clear to her it isn't going to happen." He tightened his hand around Harper's. It felt a bit awkward to discuss this in front of Harper. "But honestly I can't imagine Celeste doing something like this."

"You'd be surprised what some people will do," Dallas replied dryly. "We know somebody here in town is hiding an evil secret as far as the murders are concerned. Why wouldn't Celeste harbor a secret hatred of Harper if she was desperate enough for a date with you?" He released a deep sigh and stood. "I'll just run out to my car and get an evidence bag. I'll dust the doll for fingerprints and maybe we'll get lucky."

As he walked out the front door, Harper pulled her hand away from Sam's. "Are you okay?" he asked her worriedly.

"I will be," she replied. "I just have a few questions for Dallas." She leaned back against the sofa cushion with a frown working lines across her forehead. "I hate that we even had to bother him with this. He already has so much on his plate with the two murders that have occurred."

"True, but he also needs to know the other things that are going on in his town. I wouldn't have felt right not calling him about this," he replied.

At that moment Dallas came back through the door. "I'm assuming you don't want to keep this nasty piece of work," he said as he pulled on a pair of gloves.

"I definitely want it gone out of my house as quickly as possible," she replied fervently.

Once he had his gloves on, Dallas took the doll and placed it in the bag he'd brought in. He also put the note in the bag. "I hate to tell you this, but right now no real crime has been committed here. If things like this were to continue then I might be able to make a case for stalking or trespassing at the very least. What I hope is I can hunt down the person who did this and have a stern talk with him or her and make sure this kind of nonsense stops."

"I just want to know if I should be afraid or not," Harper said, her voice trembling slightly. Once again, a rich anger ripped through Sam. Damn whoever did this. Damn whoever had frightened her like this.

Dallas frowned thoughtfully and raked a hand through his hair. "It is a thinly veiled threat, but I don't think you need to be overly concerned with it. Honestly, people who do things like this are rarely a real physical threat. Of course, there are always exceptions to the rule, but they are rare. All I can really tell you is what I said earlier tonight at the town meeting…watch your surroundings and stay aware. Don't let anyone get into your personal space unless you want them there."

"Thank you, Dallas, for coming out here for this. I know you have far more important things to deal with right now," she said.

Dallas smiled at her. "I'm glad you called me. It's important that I know everything that's going on in this town," he said, mirroring what Sam had told her moments before.

Sam got up and walked the lawman to the door. "Thanks, Dallas. We appreciate it."

"No problem. I'll be in touch and let you know what I find out," he replied.

The minute Dallas left Sam returned to his seat

on the sofa next to Harper. "Harper, I hope you don't give this creep the power to make you stop seeing me," he said.

She stared at him for several long moments and then a slow smile curved her lips. "You know what they say about bullies. They say the best way to deal with one is to stand up to them, so I don't intend to change anything I'm doing right now."

"That's my girl," Sam replied with a smile of his own. From the moment he'd seen the doll and the note, he'd been afraid that Harper was going to tell him she was done with him.

"Are you sure you wouldn't rather date Celeste Winthrop? She's a beautiful woman and she's much more your own age," Harper said.

"Why would I want to date a woman who seems superficial and rather vacant when I can date a woman who is warm and real and can actually have a meaningful conversation with me?"

"And why would I date an old man when I can date a handsome young hunk like you?" she replied.

He was grateful to see the light back in her eyes, taking the place of the dark shadows of fear that had been there minutes before.

"I *am* totally a hunk," he replied.

She laughed. "And a humble hunk at that."

"So, we're still on for tomorrow night to go to the Farmer's Club?" he asked.

She hesitated a moment and then nodded. "Yes, we're still on."

"Then we'll firm up the time tomorrow during my lunch break."

"Sounds good to me," she replied.

He got up from the sofa. "It's getting late and I know you have an early morning so I'm going to get out of here." She got up as well and walked with him to the door.

He opened it and then turned back to her. "Are you okay to be alone tonight?"

"You'll have to work harder than that to get into my bed, Sam Bravano," she said wryly.

"No... That's... It's... That's not what I meant," he sputtered.

She laughed. "Sam, I'm just giving you a hard time, but in any case, I'll be fine. I've got good locks on my doors and windows."

"Harper, if you get scared or just feel the need to talk, no matter what the time, you know I'm only a phone call away," he said. "And I can be here in less than five minutes if you need me."

"Thank you, Sam. I really appreciate it."

He raised an eyebrow and winked at her. "Do you need a kiss to get you through the night?"

She shoved him toward the door with another laugh. "You are incorrigible. Good night, Sam."

"'Night, Harper." He stepped out on the front porch as she closed the door behind her. He waited until he heard the satisfying sound of her door lock clicking and then a dead bolt being turned.

As he walked to his truck, he used the faint light of a nearby streetlamp and the moon overhead to make sure nobody was lurking around her house.

Driving home, he tightened his hands around the steering wheel as a sharp anger stabbed into him once again. Who had left that damned mutilated doll for her to find? Who cared that much about who Harper was dating? Unfortunately, he had no idea. She had no idea, either, and he seriously doubted that Dallas would be able to find the culprit.

There was also an anger and a small amount of guilt that he was the cause of that doll being left for her. What was he supposed to do? Stop seeing her because some creep had a problem with it? Dammit, he wasn't ready to stop seeing her, especially not because of a doll and a note.

In the time he'd been working for her, he hadn't noticed anyone showing any kind of a romantic interest in her. Sure, she had several male regulars who came into the bakery, but as she'd told Dallas, none of them had ever asked her out or indicated to her that they had romance on the mind where she was concerned.

Was it possible it was some woman in town who was angry at Sam? Celeste? The woman had definitely been chasing him for the last couple of months or so. Was it possible she had done this?

Maybe when he got home, he'd find something disgusting had been left on his door, too.

He needed to call Dallas and tell him there were several other women in town who had been pretty forward in wanting Sam to ask them out. He hadn't wanted to rattle off a list of names with Harper sitting right there next to him. It would have not only been embarrassing, but it had felt like it would be disrespectful to Harper.

Despite the growing lateness of the hour, his two brothers were seated on his front porch when he pulled in and parked. "Don't you two have a home?" he asked after greeting them. He unlocked his door and the two followed him inside.

"Yeah, we have a home, but we like yours better," Michael said as he flopped down on the sofa.

"You know Ma goes to bed really early and we weren't ready to call it a night yet," Tony said as he took up the other half of the sofa.

"Why don't you move out and into your own places?" Sam eased down in his recliner, his thoughts still on Harper and what had happened. Nothing had been left on his front door which led him to believe it was somebody Harper knew who was upset about the two of them dating each other.

"You know we don't want to leave Ma all alone," Michael said.

"She would probably be happy to be all alone, and you mean you don't want to leave a place where your meals are cooked and your clothes are washed and where the two of you are babied," Sam replied.

"Well, there is that," Tony said with a laugh.

"I haven't heard from Lauren in a while. How's she doing?" Sam asked.

A touch of guilt shot through him as he thought of his older sister. Lauren was two years older than Sam and the two siblings had always been close. They usually touched base by phone at least once a week or so, but at least two weeks had gone by since the last time he'd talked to her.

"She's fine. Her and Russ have been busy putting together her shop," Tony said.

Lauren had married Russ Lincoln three years ago. Russ was a nice guy who worked as a firefighter and was helping Lauren's dream of opening a trinket and dress shop on Main Street come true.

"How's the shop coming along?" Sam asked.

"According to what Lauren told me, the interior has all been painted and the shelving is mostly in," Tony said. "You should go by and check it out. I think it's going to be really nice."

"I'll do that," Sam said.

"On another note, you'll be happy to know that Paula and I are back together again," Michael said.

"He's such a schmuck," Tony said with disgust.

"I'm happy about it if you're happy," Sam said.

"I'm totally happy," Michael said with a wide grin. "She's definitely what I want."

"Schmuck," Tony replied.

"So, what did you think about the meeting to-night?" Michael asked, obviously ignoring Tony.

"As far as I'm concerned there were no real sur-prises," Sam said.

"I feel bad for Dallas," Tony said. "He's got to be pulling his hair out over this. One murder was bad enough, but two is horrible. Sandy was a real nice woman."

"Yeah, she was, and it sounds like Dallas has no clues to help him solve the murders," Michael added.

"He's a smart man. Eventually he'll figure it out and get the murderer behind bars," Sam said.

"I found one thing very surprising about to-night," Michael said. "What are you doing with Harper Brennan?"

"I'm dating her."

Tony straightened up and stared at Sam. "For real?"

Sam nodded. "For real."

"Why?" Michael asked.

"Ah duh, because I like her," Sam said. "I like her a lot and I'm enjoying spending time with her."

"Yeah, but you could date any hot young chick in town. Why Harper? Isn't she a lot older than you?" Michael asked.

"I don't want any of the hot young chicks in town. I've already dated my share of them. Harper excites me. The age thing doesn't bother me at all. I just really like being with her," Sam said. "She's smart and funny and I'm eager to get to know her even better."

"Don't you worry that maybe she's dating you as some sort of a trophy? She must be happy for everyone to see she can score with a hot younger man," Tony replied.

That thought had crossed Sam's mind, but he knew better now. "Harper isn't that kind of a woman and right now I intend to keep seeing her whether you guys like it or not," Sam said.

"I don't have a problem with it, I just think it's kind of weird," Tony replied.

"And I give it two weeks and you'll be ready to move on to a younger, hotter woman," Michael said.

The conversation suddenly irritated him and he was glad when they didn't stay long after that. He didn't need to hear their negative opinions about dating Harper. Couldn't anyone be happy that he and Harper were happy together? And who had left that doll on her front door?

Right now, Sam had two worries in his head. The first was Harper's safety, even though he tended to agree with Dallas that the creep who'd left the doll was probably harmless.

His other concern was that Harper would bend to the pressures around her and stop seeing him. For the first time in his life, he'd found a woman he wanted to fight for and he wasn't just walking out of Harper's life without a battle.

Chapter 6

Harper checked her reflection in the mirror and mentally pronounced herself ready for another date with Sam. She'd tossed and turned all night long, thinking about the doll and her friends and Sam.

There was absolutely no way she believed Allie or Becky had anything to do with the doll. They'd certainly speak their minds, and had during the meeting, but Harper believed there was no way they'd stoop to such a level as to leave that horrendous doll for her to find. They just weren't that kind of people.

The easy thing for her to do would be to stop seeing Sam in any kind of a social way. Then her friends would be happy and whoever had left the doll for her would be happy. Everyone would be happy except her.

That day when Sam had taken his lunchtime inside the bakery with her, he'd reminded her of just how much she enjoyed his company. He caused a girly breathlessness deep inside her at the same time he made her laugh.

His presence in her life had eased the deep core of loneliness that had been with her since the day her husband had walked out on her. And somehow, she didn't believe anyone else would have done that as well as Sam had.

All the pushback she had gotten about dating him had made her wake up that morning with a new determination that she was going to see Sam whenever, however she damn well pleased. To heck with everyone else.

She wasn't a complete fool. She didn't believe they had any kind of a real future together, but for the first time in her life, she was doing something to please herself. He made her happy, and she hadn't really been happy in her personal life in a very long time. She would continue to see Sam as long as he wanted to see her.

She now left her bathroom and went into the living room to wait for Sam's arrival. It was going to be a very low-key night, drinks and conversation at the Farmer's Club. After last night she was definitely looking for a low-key, drama-free evening.

It had been another hot day and so she wore another sundress this evening, this time in a bright pink. She'd worn it several times before and had always gotten compliments, so she knew it looked good on her. And she wanted to look as good as she could for Sam.

She jumped up as a knock sounded on the door. That would be him and her heart did a crazy little dance as she went to answer. She opened the door and a new warmth swept through her at the sight of him. Nobody wore a pair of jeans as well as Sam, and the emerald green polo shirt he wore brought out the beautiful color of his long-lashed eyes. He looked totally hot.

That charming dimple winked in his cheek as he grinned at her. "Wow, you look absolutely gorgeous," he said as his gaze swept the length of her. It wasn't just his words, but the light in his eyes that heated the pool of warmth that was already in her stomach. His eyes told her that his words were true. He really thought she looked gorgeous.

"Thank you, and you clean up real nice, too," she replied.

She stepped out into the warm evening air and after locking her door, together they headed for his truck. Gray clouds overhead portended the possibility of a rainstorm. She knew the farmers in the area were probably hoping for rain after the past couple weeks of unrelentingly hot days.

"The bakery is looking better and better every day," she said once they were in his truck.

He smiled. "Yeah, it won't be long now before it's ready for a fresh coat of paint. Have you thought about what color you'd like?"

"Something bright and fun. I'm thinking maybe a cheerful yellow," she replied.

He laughed. "I was sure you were going to tell me you wanted it painted a hot pink."

She also laughed. "Trust me, I considered it, but in the end, I decided I don't want a big pink building."

"Yellow would be nice, and some of the trim could be pink."

"That sounds perfect," she replied, glad that they were on the same page. "The building would look like one of my lemon cupcakes."

"You still need to show me what you want in the back of the building," he reminded her.

Instantly, a vision of Sandy Blackstone on a pole with her eyes gone and her mouth sewn shut with thick black thread sprang into her head. The idea of going out into the backyard again still filled her with a deep anxiety.

"Sooner or later, you've got to go back out there," Sam said softly, as if reading her thoughts. He reached out and lightly touched her hand. "We'll make something really beautiful out there." He returned his hand to the steering wheel.

Once again, her heart warmed with his words. He always seemed to know exactly what to say to make her feel better. He always seemed to know what was important to her. Sam was definitely getting under her skin and the last thing she wanted was for him to get into her heart. That would definitely make her a foolish old woman.

He pulled up and parked in front of the Farmer's Club. The bar was located in a small building just off Main Street. The front of the bar was quite unassuming, with blinds in the windows and one small neon beer sign.

He helped her out of the truck and then they entered the bar. Instantly her nose was assailed by the scents of frying onions, hamburgers and beer.

There was a long, polished bar on one side of the room and booths and tables on the other. Along the back was a dartboard and a shuffleboard area where two older couples were currently playing.

She was surprised that Sam was greeted not only by several of the old men seated at the bar, but also by the bartender, Ranger Simmons. He also greeted her, as he was one of her morning regulars.

She knew that Ranger had lost his wife years ago. He had a farm on the outskirts of town that he had ultimately given to his son. He'd been the owner of this place for over twenty years and now lived alone in the rooms upstairs.

Sam led her to an empty booth and once they settled in, Ranger walked over to them to take their orders. "Hey, Harper, you look really nice tonight. That pink is really your color."

"Thanks, Ranger," she replied with a smile.

"She looks good in any color," Sam said.

"That's true, and the bakery is looking better already," Ranger said.

"That's thanks to Sam," she replied with a warm look across the table.

"You'd better do right by her, Sam," Ranger said.

Sam laughed. "I know if I don't, I'll have to answer to all the regular customers she has."

"You got that right," Ranger replied with a laugh of his own. "Now, what would the lady like this evening?" he asked.

Harper wasn't really much of a drinker, but occasionally she enjoyed a beer or a gin and tonic, so she ordered the latter. "With a double twist of lime," she added.

Ranger smiled at her. "Ah, a perfect drink for a hot summer night. What about you, Sam? The usual?"

"That works for me," Sam replied.

"Any food for the two of you?" Ranger asked.

Sam looked at Harper. "Please, order anything you like. Ranger is a master of all kinds of bar food."

"Thanks, but I'm good for now," she replied. She had eaten a sandwich before Sam had picked her up. She especially felt good right now given the fact that nobody in the bar had looked at them askance. In fact, several of the other couples had nodded and smiled at them pleasantly. It was definitely a nice change from their night in the café.

Within minutes they both had their drinks and she discovered Sam's regular was a whisky and soda. The music playing overhead was soft, an old George Jones country tune, and the other conversations in the room were nothing more than soft murmurs.

"Do you come here often?" she asked.

"Not too often, but occasionally. It's a good place to come alone and unwind with a drink. Of course, it's much nicer to have you here to unwind with," he said with that smile that always melted something deep inside her.

"I'm glad to be here with you," she replied.

"Sometimes I enjoy coming here and sitting with some of the old-timers. I like talking to them about a variety of topics," he said.

For the next few minutes, they talked about the work on the bakery and some things she would like to see in the backyard behind it.

"I want a nice covered patio where on nice days families can come and sit and enjoy the ambiance along with the food," she said. "I'll run different kinds of family specials that will hopefully bring in more people."

"That's one of the things I admire about you, you're a smart businesswoman," he said.

She laughed. "I'll tell you a little secret. I mostly fly by the seat of my pants."

"Then you have darn good instincts," he replied. "My brothers and I have our own business, the Bravano Brothers Renovation and Construction Company."

She looked at him in surprise. "I didn't realize you all were an actual company. I just thought you and your brothers casually worked with each other."

"I know that's how it appears, but we are an actual LLC company. I keep the books. Everything that we make goes into the business bank account and then we pay ourselves out of that."

"I've seen your brothers working on the gazebo in the park." She took a sip of her drink. "It looks like that's going to be beautiful for everyone to enjoy."

He nodded. "It is going to be nice. They should be finished with that job just in time to help me at the bakery."

"You seem to have plenty to do around town."

"We stay really busy during the summers. The buildings in this town need a lot of work and there seems to be a general mood among the building owners that now is the time to renew things."

"And then what will you do when everything is done here in Millsville?" she asked curiously.

"I figure by that time I'll be ready to retire. Then I'll be your houseboy and clean and cook for you and eat delicious cakes every night," he said with that charming twinkle in his eyes.

She laughed. "It's nice to know you have your future all planned out for yourself."

He took a drink and then gazed into her eyes once again. "What do you see for your future?"

"To be honest, I don't think about my future too much. I tend to live in the here and now," she replied and then took a sip of her drink.

"But if you were to really think about it right now, what do you foresee for yourself?" He leaned forward slightly and his gaze seemed to be probing deep inside her.

"Oh, I don't know. I'd like to work the bakery for a long time and then maybe when it's at the very height of being profitable, I'd sell it and live on the proceeds."

"And then what? Do you see yourself traveling or writing a book, or just swinging in a hammock?" he asked.

"Definitely not swinging in a hammock or writing a book, but a little traveling would be nice. I've never been out of Millsville," she said.

"Ever?" he asked in surprise. "Didn't you and your ex-husband ever travel on a vacation?"

"My ex-husband's idea of a vacation was to drive out to Johnson's pond and go fishing," she replied. Ed Johnson lived on a farm on the outskirts of town and had the biggest, best fishing pond in the area. He was a cantankerous old widower who charged people for fishing privileges.

"Then we have to plan to take a trip together,"

he said, the twinkle back in his eyes. "Where would you like to go for your first trip out of Millsville?"

"Oh, I'd love to fly to New York City and visit Times Square, or maybe jet off to Las Vegas and try my hand at the tables." She laughed. "If we're really fantasizing here, why not a quick trip to the Bahamas or another beautiful island. Have you traveled a lot?"

"Not a whole lot, but I've done some. I've been to New York City and to San Francisco. I've also been to the Grand Canyon and to Niagara Falls. However, I've never been out of the country. There's so much to see and explore right here in the United States."

"I definitely agree with that. I've just never felt like I could close up shop and take any real time off," she replied.

"But you should. At least once a year you should close down for a week or so and get out of town. It would be good for you and the people of Millsville will survive without their cake and cookies for a week. I've never been to Las Vegas. Maybe sometime in the future we could plan a trip together there."

She smiled. "We'll see," she replied. However, the idea of traveling somewhere, anywhere with Sam was incredibly appealing. Part of the reason she'd never traveled anywhere was because her husband had never wanted to and then after he left her, she didn't go anywhere because she was a woman all alone.

Now her head filled with visions of her and Sam walking hand in hand down the Vegas strip. They would gamble a little bit during the day and then they could eat dinner together in a castle or some other fun restaurant. Then they would head back to a hotel room where they would...

She stopped the thoughts before they could take her to a place where she'd blush and fill with a heat to rival one of her hot flashes.

He ordered another round of drinks for them and the topic of conversation went back to family. "If you don't mind my asking, why didn't you and your husband ever have any children?" he asked.

"My husband never wanted children and to be honest, I wasn't one of those maternal women who wanted to get married and have babies. I spent a lot of my marriage working hard to save money to open up the bakery. That's my child." She paused and took another drink, then gazed at him once again. "Do you want to have children?"

He smiled. "No, I've never been one of those paternal men who wanted to get married and have babies. Having children just isn't in my wheelhouse."

"Are you sure you won't change your mind about that in the future?" she pressed. This was definitely an issue that concerned her if she and Sam were to continue having a relationship. She couldn't give him a child if that was what he wanted. Of course, she still didn't believe there was any kind of a future with him, especially that kind of a long-term future.

"I'm positive, although I'm looking forward to being an uncle to my siblings' children." There was a note of finality in his voice. "And now I want to ask you a very important question."

"Wait, if it's a very important question then I'd better have another sip of this." She picked up her glass and took a big gulp, then looked at him with a touch of anxiety.

He laughed. "It's not that important, Harper. I just wanted to know if this Sunday you'd come over to my mom's house and have dinner with my family. I'd really love for you to meet everyone."

"Oh, I don't know," she replied and took another sip of her drink. The idea of meeting his family was more than a little bit daunting.

"Come on, Harper. I promise you none of us bite and Mom is making her eggplant parmesan, which is absolutely delicious. You can officially meet my mom, my brothers and my sister and they can meet you."

"Sister?" She looked at him in surprise. "I didn't know you had a sister. You've never talked about her before."

He nodded. "Yeah, Lauren. She's two years older than me and happily married. Now, don't change the subject. Will you come to dinner on

Sunday? I'll pick you up and take you back home." He reached across the table and took her hand in his. "It's important to me, Harper. I'd really like for you to come."

Oh, his green eyes pulled her in and as always, the touch of his hand around hers both thrilled her and made her feel oddly safe. "Okay," she relented. "I suppose I'll come."

His dimple winked as he gave her a huge smile. "That's my girl." He squeezed her hand and then released it.

She released a deep sigh. "I wish I could introduce you to my parents. My father would have liked you."

"And your mother wouldn't have liked me?" One of his dark eyebrows shot up.

"Oh, no…she would have liked you, too. But my father and you would have had a lot in common. Even though he worked as a janitor at the high school, he liked to do a little woodworking on the weekends."

"I'm sorry I can't meet them," he said softly. Once again, he reached out, took her hand in his and gently squeezed.

"Yeah, me too," she replied and cast him a bittersweet smile.

It was just after ten when they left the Farmer's Club. By the time they left, Harper had a little buzz on and she wasn't sure if it was from the two drinks she had consumed or from having Sam's undivided attention for so long.

He definitely had the ability to make a woman feel like she was the most important, most beautiful woman in the room. He made her feel witty and smart. It was a heady feeling and one she had never experienced from a man before.

Her husband had been a rather cold man, short on compliments and even shorter on attention and affection. Looking back now, she wasn't even sure why she had married him. She must have loved him at one time, but after the affair it was now difficult to tap back into any loving feelings she might have once had for him.

Sam was a whole different kind of animal. He was gregarious and attentive. He was affectionate and caring and he filled a hole inside her soul that she hadn't even known was there.

"I've enjoyed this evening, Harper," he said as he walked her to her front door.

"I really enjoyed it, too. Thank you for inviting me," she replied. She unlocked her front door and then turned back to him.

"I'll pick you up on Sunday about noon, and we usually eat about one or so," he said. Lightning flashed in the distance, followed by a low rumble of thunder.

"Okay, now you better get out of here before you get wet," she said with a glance up at the thick clouds overhead.

LOYAL READER
FREE BOOKS VOUCHER
WELCOME BOX

YES! I Love Reading, please send me a welcome box with up to 4 FREE BOOKS and Free Mystery Gifts from the series I select.

Just write in "YES" on the dotted line below then return this card today and we'll send your welcome box asap!

➡️ YES ⬅️

Which do you prefer?

| ☐ **Harlequin® Romantic Suspense** 240/340 HDL GRTY | ☐ **Harlequin Intrigue® Larger-Print** 199/399 HDL GRTY | ☐ **BOTH** 240/340 & 199/399 HDL GQ93 |

FIRST NAME   LAST NAME

ADDRESS

APT.#   CITY

STATE/PROV.   ZIP/POSTAL CODE

EMAIL ☐ Please check this box if you would like to receive newsletters and promotional emails from Harlequin Enterprises ULC and its affiliates. You can unsubscribe anytime.

HI/HRS-622-LR_LRV22

He grinned at her. "A little rain never hurt me. Besides, before I leave, I'm hoping to get a good-night kiss."

Her heartbeat quickened as he leaned closer to her, so close she could feel his body heat and see the tiny gold flecks in the very depths of his green eyes. "So, am I going to leave here brokenhearted or are you going to let me kiss you good-night?"

She laughed. "Oh, jeez, you're so dramatic. I certainly don't want to be the one to break your heart."

He immediately drew her into his arms and claimed her lips with his. She opened her mouth to him and their tongues moved together in a heated dance.

As the kiss continued, she reached up and wrapped her arms around his neck and he pulled her intimately close against him. She loved the feel of his strong, broad chest against her breasts and the fire that had ignited inside her grew more intense.

He finally pulled his lips from hers and blazed a trail of teasing nips and kisses down her throat. She threw her head back to allow him access. She was lost…utterly lost in the desire he stoked inside her.

It had been so long since a man had held her so tightly, so long since she'd experienced the fluttering heat that now rushed through her.

It was him who finally released her and took a

step backward. His eyes glittered hot with desire and he swept a hand through his hair. "Oh, woman. You are so in my blood." His words shot another rivulet of delicious heat through her.

At that moment the skies opened up and rain began to pour down on them. "Go, get inside before you drown," he said with a laugh.

"Good night, Sam. I'll see you tomorrow," she replied and then hurried through her door.

However, she didn't see him the next morning. The rain system that had moved in the night before had stalled overhead and rain continued to fall the next day.

Just because Sam couldn't work didn't mean he was out of her thoughts. In fact, he was all she could think about as she baked her goods for the day and then opened the bakery for business.

Things seemed to be moving incredibly fast with Sam. There had been a moment at the door the night before while he was kissing her that she'd actually considered letting him come inside to make love with her.

Her intense desire for him had shocked and surprised her. That desire wasn't just built on the fact that Sam was good-looking and had an awesome body. Rather she wanted him because he was a good man who drew her in emotionally as well as physically.

She also knew now that he desired her. Last night as he'd pulled her so tight against his body, she'd realized that he was fully aroused. That had only made her desire for him grow hotter and more intense.

And this Sunday she was going to meet all his family. Yes, everything with Sam was definitely moving fast. She still had no idea where things were going with him or how long they would be going at all. Right now, she was just thoroughly enjoying the ride.

Surely there would come a time when Sam would realize she was too old, much too staid for him. Surely he would eventually tire of her company and want someone livelier...somebody younger. She knew that time would eventually come and that was why she needed to hang on to her heart where he was concerned.

She was just enjoying Sam's company and having fun, she kept telling herself, and she assumed that was what he was doing with her as well. But when the fun was over, she knew he'd move on.

Could she sleep with him and still hang on to her heart? She believed she could. Was she ready to take that next step with him? She wasn't sure.

The dreary, rainy morning kept everyone away from the bakery. Even her regulars didn't show up for their usual coffee and cinnamon rolls as rain pelted down from the gray skies.

It was early afternoon when Sam called her. "What's happening with my favorite baker?" he

asked, his deep voice rolling over her in pleasant tones.

"Absolutely nothing," she replied. "Not a single
soul has been inside this morning."

"Really? That's unusual," he replied.

"It's just too rainy for anyone to want to get
out."

"Do you miss me?"

"I plead the Fifth," she said with a laugh.

"There you go again, playing hard to get."

She laughed again. The truth was she did miss
him. Even though he worked outside, it was always
nice to know he was there. It was definitely nice
to watch him work. She was going to miss him in
the next hour or so when he normally came inside
for his break.

"What are you doing today?" she asked.

"I'm moping around."

She laughed. "You are not."

"Okay, I'm not. I just got finished painting the
bathroom in the basement."

"I knew you were probably working on something. You aren't one to just sit idle for too long."

"If you've been there all alone all morning
that means you've had a lot of time to think. You
haven't changed your mind about Sunday, have
you?" he asked.

"No, I haven't changed my mind," she replied.

"Good, I'm really looking forward to it. I know
my family is going to love you."

"I hope so." A wave of anxiety swept through her as she thought about spending the day with his family.

They chatted for a little while longer and then said their goodbyes. Hopefully the weather would be better by tomorrow and Sam would be back working as usual.

At around two o'clock the rain finally stopped, but the clouds remained thick and gray overhead. It was just after two when Annie Cook came through the door. Annie was a pleasant young woman who had two children, and she frequented the bakery often.

"What a miserable, dreary day it has been," she said as she came through the door. "How are you doing, Harper?"

"I'm about to die of boredom. It's been a very slow day. In fact, you're my first customer of the day," Harper replied.

"Oh, wow, you probably have been bored in here all by yourself. It's been such a dismal day I decided to treat my kids and hubby with some cupcakes," Annie said.

"What kind would you like? I have chocolate, vanilla, and dark cherry ones today," Harper explained.

"How about two of each," Annie replied.

"How are your kids doing?" Harper asked as she began boxing up the cupcakes.

"Right now, they're at my mother's for a little

while. I love my kids, but to be perfectly honest I'm more than ready for summer to be over and school to begin."

Harper laughed. "I imagine all the mothers in town are feeling that way about now."

"Especially on rainy days like today," Annie added. "My little angels suddenly turn into little monsters when they're cooped up inside for too long." Annie pulled money out of her wallet. "I definitely needed a little break from them. I should feel guilty that I dropped them off at my mother's earlier, but do you want to know a secret? I don't feel guilty at all."

Harper laughed again. "I promise your secret is safe with me."

A few minutes after Annie left, RJ Morgan strode into the bakery. RJ owned the tattoo shop next door. He was a walking advertisement for his business. His bald head and face were heavily inked, as were his thick arms. He was a big, burly man who Harper had always found rather intimidating.

"Hi, RJ," she said with a smile. He'd only been in the shop once before and that had been when she'd first bought the building and, on that day, he had been very angry. Apparently one of his buddies had intended to buy the bakery building and he'd been angry that she'd bought it before his friend could get all his finances together.

He didn't return her smile. "Harper, when is all the crap you have outside going to be cleaned up?"

She took a step backward, surprised at the question. "As soon as Sam Bravano is finished with renovating the front of the bakery," she replied.

"There's so much crap, it's a damn eyesore out there," he replied, his brow pulled down to his bushy eyebrows in a deep frown. He was half leaning over the display counter, slightly menacing in his nearness.

"It's all the materials Sam is using to do the job," she countered.

"Why can't he put them out around the back where they can't be seen?"

"Why would he do that when he's using them on the front of the building?" she replied.

"He'd better use them up damn fast. I'm sick of seeing it all."

Harper raised her chin defensively. "It's on my property and it can be there as long as it needs to be." A hot flash suddenly took hold of her, heating her face, her neck and her chest.

She knew her face was probably turning a beet red as small dots of sweat sprang out on her forehead. "Nothing is on your property or bothering your business, so you have no right to complain about anything."

Her voice might have sounded more strident than she intended, for RJ took a step backward. Or maybe he moved back because he saw her turning bright red and he was afraid she might explode.

"If any of that material gets on my property, I'll burn it," he said and then turned and exited the shop.

Harper released a deep sigh and then hurried over to the sink. She wet an unused cleaning cloth and wiped it across her face and neck in an effort to cool down.

The hot flash slowly passed and as usual left her slightly chilled. She sat on the chair behind the cash register, wrapped her arms around herself and released another deep sigh.

RJ was a total jerk. There was no way the material Sam had stacked outside her store in any way affected the business in the tattoo shop next door. He'd been mad at her ever since she'd bought the building. He must have just been waiting all this time for something to bitch to her about.

At four-thirty a light rain started up again and Harper began to get things ready to close. She put the items that froze well into the freezer and then packed up some of the other things for Elijah Simpson to pick up.

Every Wednesday he came in for any of her leftovers for the food bank he ran out of the basement of his house. She knew there were some people in town and around the area who sometimes went to bed hungry, and that absolutely broke her heart.

Even though she only had sweets, she was always happy to give Elijah whatever she could.

At ten 'til five, Elijah came through her door. He was a tall, thin Black man with salt-and-pepper hair, a wide, warm smile, and a kind and gentle spirit.

"Hey, Elijah, how's it going?" she greeted him with a smile.

"It's going okay," he replied. "How are you doing, Harper?"

"Okay, although I've decided I hate rainy days."

He laughed. "Most of us do, but the farmers in the area will be happy with all this rain. They've definitely needed it lately." He eyed her for a long moment and then grinned. "I've been hearing that besides the latest murder, you're causing a bit of a stir on the gossip scene."

Harper sighed. "Apparently so. It's amazing how many people in this town are interested in my personal life."

"It's probably not that many but rather just a loud few," he replied.

"Are you going to tell me what a foolish old woman I am?"

Elijah laughed. "First of all, you aren't an old woman. Secondly, what I'll tell you is to do what makes you happy. Life is far too short, and lately, too full of sadness, not to try to find your own little piece of happiness. And once you find that, don't let anyone take it away from you."

"Thank you, Elijah. That's exactly what I believe and I'm trying to ignore all the naysayers," she replied.

"That's exactly what you should do," he said.

"Now, I've got two big bags for you today." She bent down to retrieve the things she'd packed up for him and then placed them on the counter.

"God bless you, Harper. I always try to make sure your items go to the families with children so that occasionally they can get a little sweet treat."

"I'm just glad it helps," she said.

"Oh, it helps. Every little bit helps," he replied. "And I thank you for what you donate to me."

Minutes later Elijah was gone and Harper turned the sign in the door to Closed. She was glad to close up after the long, boring day. Hopefully tomorrow the rain would be gone and business would be better.

Thank goodness she had driven her car this morning for it was raining once again and a preternatural darkness had fallen outside.

Once she'd set up things in the kitchen for the next morning, she pulled on the lightweight yellow raincoat she'd worn that morning and then went out the front door. She locked it behind her and then ran to her car parked along the side of the building.

The police had finally finished up with their investigation and released the backyard to her. However, she still hadn't made herself venture back out there yet. She just hadn't been able to force herself to go back there.

Visions of Sandy once again filled her head. She tried not to think about what she had seen, but occasionally unbidden thoughts of the horror sprang into her mind. She now consciously pushed the horrible images out of her head.

Once inside her vehicle, she shook her head and brushed the raindrops off her shoulders and then put the key in the ignition. She turned the key.

Nothing. No roar of the motor, not even an ominous click. She tried it once again with the same results. *Oh jeez*, she thought. *What now?* She waited several minutes and then tried it again. Still nothing. Obviously, the car wasn't going to start.

Damn. The rain continued to patter down on her car windows. Of all the evenings to have car trouble, she thought with a sigh. She was certainly no mechanic, but it sounded like a dead battery and she was in no mood to sit around and wait for somebody from the garage to come and jump her.

Her house was only a block and a half away. She could run home and call somebody to take care of the car in the morning. A little rain certainly wouldn't hurt her.

She sat for a few minutes longer and thankfully the rain turned into a heavy mist. Decision made, she opened her car door and stepped out.

At least the mist wasn't cold, but rather refreshingly cool. Still, she put her head down and walked briskly. Hopefully the car issue really was just the battery and would be a quick fix in the morning.

A dog barked nearby and a squirrel raced across the sidewalk in front of her. She thought she heard a footstep behind her and she stopped and turned around as the hairs on the nape of her neck raised up.

There was nobody behind her on the sidewalk. All she saw were the dark shadows that the clouds overhead had created. She turned back around and continued her brisk walk.

She was grateful to reach her front door. She now felt soaked and chilled throughout and a touch of uneasiness had risen up inside her. She inserted her key and unlocked the door and then gasped as somebody grabbed her by her shoulder and spun her around.

For a brief moment she couldn't comprehend what was happening. A man faced her. He wore dark pants, a black shirt and a ski mask that disguised his identity.

"Bitch," he hissed and then shot out a fist. She saw the glitter of the knife blade in his hand at the last minute and with a gasp, she whirled to the side.

The knife slashed through her thin raincoat and pain seared through her shoulder where the knife had glanced off. Terror slammed into her, tightening the back of her throat and making it impossible for her to draw a breath, let alone scream.

What was happening? Her brain struggled to

make sense of it. Who was this man? Even as those questions flew through her head, she knew they didn't matter. She was in imminent danger.

Get away. Run! an inner voice screamed inside her head, but he had her trapped with her back against her door and with nowhere to go. He stabbed at her again…and once again she managed to deflect it from hitting anything vital on her body. Still, the knife sliced into her forearm and again a searing pain roared through her.

He continued to slash at her, cutting her over and over as she did her best to dodge and weave away from the knife. Tears of pain…of terror blurred her eyes as she continued to twist and turn to escape a deadly stab.

Fight back, the voice screeched inside her. *If you can't run…then fight*, the voice continued. Sooner or later his knife would do deadly damage to her if she didn't do something, anything to stop him. She needed to act. She needed to do something to get herself out of this dangerous situation.

She finally found her voice and began to scream as loud as she possibly could. As she continued to shriek for help, a porch light blinked on across the street. A frisson of relief swept through her as she realized her screams were being heard.

The attacker paused for a brief moment and shot a glance across the street. She took the opportunity and slammed her knee up, catching him hard between his legs. He grunted and stumbled backward a step. While he was off balance, she shoved him with all the strength she could muster. He fell off the front porch and to the ground. He roared in obvious rage.

In a frantic panic, she quickly turned to her door where the keys still hung in the lock. She yanked them out, opened the door and ran inside. She immediately slammed the door behind her and locked it.

Leaning with her back against the door, she tried to catch her breath even as deep, frantic sobs ripped through her. Oh, God, what had just happened? Who was that person?

She remained against the door only a moment. She ran to her front window and pulled the curtain aside. She looked all around but there was nobody there. Apparently, her attacker had melted back into the mist and out of sight.

Who was he? Why had he attacked her? More importantly, was he still out there and would he try to get in to finish the job he'd started?

Chapter 7

"Sam, I… I need you." Harper's voice trembled as it came across the phone line. It was obvious she was half sobbing and that was all he needed to hear from her.

"I'll be right over." He disconnected the call, grabbed his wallet and keys and then flew out of his house. He had no idea what was going on, but it must be something drastic for Harper to call him in tears.

I need you. Her words resonated deep inside him. He drove like a bat out of hell, his heart beating a frantic rhythm. What was going on? What had happened? Dammit, he should have asked her some more questions before he'd disconnected the call.

The rain had finally stopped, but he had to slow

down several times for standing puddles in the road. The wind had picked up, sending leaves and errant trash flying through the air.

When he finally turned onto the street where Harper's house was located his heart fell to the pit of his stomach as he saw Dallas's car parked in the driveway. What on earth had happened with her that required the chief of police to respond?

Sam pulled up behind the police car and flew out of his truck. He raced for the front door and when he reached it, he didn't bother to knock. He stepped inside and when Harper saw him, she jumped up from the sofa and flew into his arms. She sobbed with her face buried in his chest as he threw a questioning look at Dallas.

"Harper's car didn't start tonight when she was ready to leave the bakery, so she decided to walk home. She got to her front door and somebody attacked her," Dallas said.

"Attacked her?" Sam echoed in stunned surprise.

"He…he tried to kill me," Harper said amid sobs. "Sam, he t-tried to st-stab me to death."

"She has several places where he managed to slice her up," Dallas said. "I've got an ambulance coming so one of the EMTs can check her out. She insisted she didn't want to go to the emergency room."

Outrage swept through Sam as he led Harper to the sofa. He pulled her down to sit next to him as she finally stopped crying. For the first time Sam saw the slashes in her raincoat sleeves and the blood that still looked wet and sticky.

"Who in the hell did this to her?" Sam asked angrily.

"I was just about to ask Harper some questions when you came in," Dallas said. He sat in the chair facing the sofa.

As he began to interview Harper on the details of the attacker, it quickly became clear that there would be no way for Dallas or anyone else to identify who it had been.

The only information Harper could give Dallas was that the attacker was male. "It all happened so fast. I'm sorry, but I can't even tell you how tall he was or what kind of body type he had. I was too busy trying to keep him from stabbing me in the stomach or chest to pay any attention to anything else."

Sam pulled her closer against his side, his outrage and anger morphing into a fierce protective mode and abject fear for her. Somebody had tried to kill her tonight and what scared him was that there was a very strong possibility that he would try to kill her again. And the next time he might be successful.

"Did this person say anything to you?" Dallas asked.

"No...uh...yes," she replied. "He called me a

bitch right before he tried to stab me for the first time."

"I'm assuming you didn't recognize the voice." Dallas said it as a statement.

She shook her head negatively, looking positively miserable. "It was just a gravelly hiss. I would never be able to recognize it again unless I heard him say it exactly the same way."

"Have you had any problems with anyone lately, Harper?" Dallas asked. "Aside from the doll that was left for you? Has anything else happened that disturbed you in any way? Maybe something concerning your interactions at the bakery?"

"No…uh, maybe a little," she replied. As she told Dallas about her encounter that day with RJ Morgan, Sam began to fist and unfist his hands.

"If RJ had a problem with my lumber and other supplies, he should have come and talked about it with me," Sam said, unable to hide the anger in his voice. "Dammit, he should have never brought it to Harper."

"You leave RJ to me," Dallas replied with a warning glance at him. "Anything else you can tell me, Harper?" he asked her.

"No, I think I've told you everything." Tears once again filled her eyes.

At that moment the ambulance arrived and Andy Unger and George Ingram, both EMTs, came inside. As Sam watched them tend to Harper's various cuts, his anger once again rose up.

Who had slashed her up like this? Who had hurt her like this? Dammit, he'd like to find the person responsible for wounding her...for attacking her, and beat his ass good right before Dallas arrested him.

Thankfully Andy and George both agreed she needed no further treatment after she indicated her tetanus shot was up to date, and then they left.

"I'm sorry to say, but I'll need your clothes, Harper," Dallas said. "Can you go change into something else and give me your blouse and slacks for evidence?"

"Of course," she replied. "They're all ruined anyway."

He gestured toward the raincoat she'd already removed so her wounds could be tended to. "I'll have to take your raincoat as well."

"That's okay. It's of no use to me anymore." She got up and left the room and went into what Sam assumed was her bedroom.

"Dallas, what in the hell is going on?" Sam said the minute he heard Harper's bedroom door close.

Dallas raked a hand through his curly dark hair. "I wish I knew who the hell was responsible for this attack."

"She didn't give you much to go on," Sam said.

"She didn't give me anything to go on." Dallas released a deep sigh. "I'm going to scour the area around her front door to see if I can find something...anything that might help me identify this perp. I'll be interviewing more people and checking with the neighbors to see if they saw anyone hanging around here before and during the attack. She told me that the neighbors across the street turned on their porch light when she started to scream. I'm hoping they'll be able to help. I've also got several of my men checking out the neighborhood, looking for anyone who might be lurking around."

"I hope you find something," Sam replied.

"If she hadn't managed to get into the house when she did, I'd be here investigating her murder," Dallas said darkly.

His words caused a chill to race up and down Sam's spine.

"Do you think it's possible it was the Scarecrow Killer?"

"Anything is possible," Dallas replied. "If it was, then he's changed his victim profile. Harper isn't a blonde."

At that moment Harper returned to the room. She was now clad in a long soft-looking blue robe and looked small and vulnerable. She handed Dallas her clothing and he placed it in a brown paper evidence bag. She then sank back down on the sofa next to Sam, who put his arm around her and drew her close to his side.

Thirty minutes later Dallas had left and Sam remained on the sofa holding Harper. "I'm so sorry this happened to you, Harper," he said softly. "I'm so sorry, baby, and I'm so damned angry about it all."

She stirred from his arms and sat back from him. "I'm so scared and I'm so confused. Who would want to hurt me that badly? Who wants to kill me, Sam? What on earth have I done to anger somebody so much?"

Her big blue eyes filled with the mist of tears and her face was still unnaturally pale. He positively ached for her. "Baby, I wish I knew. I'll tell you one thing...until Dallas has the person under arrest, I intend to protect you twenty-four hours a day."

"I appreciate the sentiment, but how do you intend to do that?" She looked at him curiously, hopefully.

"I'm moving in here." He didn't know when he had made that decision, but he felt as if that was the only way to make sure she remained safe. It felt like the right thing to do. "Harper, I'll sleep on the sofa, or I'll sleep on the floor, but I can't just go home and leave you vulnerable here."

She stared at him for several long moments. "My first instinct is to tell you no, that it's absolutely not necessary. But the truth is I'm scared, and having you here, at least for a little while, would definitely make me feel much better."

"Then it's all settled. I'll stay tonight, and tomorrow after work you can go with me to my place so I can pack up a few things." He was grateful to see that some of the color had returned to her face.

"It's going to be okay, Harper." He pulled her back into his arms. She relaxed against him and released a deep, shuddery sigh.

"I don't know what I'd do without you," she said softly. "And I can't believe you're going to disrupt your own life for me."

"Don't you get it, Harper?" He leaned back from her and gazed into her eyes. "I care about you deeply and more than anything I want to be here for you."

She lingered in his arms for several quiet moments and then she sat up and moved away from him. "I want to go take a shower. I need to erase the feel of that man touching me when he was trying to stab me. Right now, I just feel so dirty."

He frowned. "Are you sure you should do that with the bandages that Amos and George put on you?"

She nodded. "I've got the supplies to replace them once I feel clean, and I really need to get clean." She got to her feet. "Make yourself at home. The television remote is there on the coffee table." She gave him a wan smile. "This shouldn't take me too long."

"Don't worry about me." He shot her a reassuring smile. "I'll be right here when you get out of the shower."

The minute she left the room, his smile died

on his lips. Staying with her here wasn't a problem for him. There was nothing to tie him to his home, no pets to take care of or plants to water or anyone to answer to.

There was no way he would leave Harper alone with some madman trying to kill her. Once again, a rush of adrenaline fueled by anger ripped through him. Who in the hell was behind the attack? Who hated Harper enough to want her dead? God, he wished he had the answer.

Was it possible it had been the Scarecrow Killer who had attacked her tonight? They had no idea how the murderer got his victims. However, he knew that Sandy hadn't been slashed up all over like that. Her knife wounds were only in her stomach.

When he'd seen the bloody cuts on Harper's arms and shoulder and thought about the terror she must have felt in that moment, he'd seriously wanted to hurt somebody.

Why was this happening to her? She was pleasant and kind to everyone who came into the bakery. He'd never seen or heard about her having a cross word with anyone.

He got up from the sofa and began to pace the living room floor, his stomach tied in tense knots as his brain worked to somehow make sense of what had happened.

Then he remembered the doll and the note. Oh, God, he'd been so stupid. It hadn't been the Scarecrow Killer. She'd been warned before with the doll and note. He was the reason this was happening to her. Why hadn't he seen it before now? It was so apparent. The doll had been her warning against dating him, but she hadn't heeded the warning. This was all about him…about her dating him. His heart plunged to the floor.

If he stopped seeing her would the danger immediately go away? Right now, he couldn't imagine her not being a part of his life, but if he had to distance himself from her in order to keep her safe from harm, he would do it in a minute. Not because he wanted to, but because he cared enough about her to leave her.

He sank back down on the sofa and thought about the tough conversation he needed to have with her when she got out of the shower.

Harper stood in the shower and once again hot tears mingled with the warm water. The cuts on her arms and shoulders burned beneath the spray, but that wasn't what caused her tears. Even though the wounds hurt, they were all fairly superficial.

She still couldn't believe what had happened to her. Who was the person who had attacked her? What would have happened if she hadn't been able to fight him off? What would have happened if she hadn't managed to get through her front door and lock it behind her? She knew the answer to that last question.

She'd be dead.

There was no question in her mind that he would have managed to stab her to death. That thought terrified her. Despite the heat of the water even more icy chills raced up and down her back. Thank God for Sam. There was no question she'd feel safer with him in her house.

She felt perfectly safe when she was at work at the bakery, whether Sam was outside or not. That was a public place with people coming in and out on a fairly regular basis. She couldn't imagine anyone trying to attack her there.

It was here, in her home, that for the first time since her divorce she was afraid to be alone. It was thoughts of Sam that made her tears finally halt.

She had no idea what it would be like to have him around the house all the time…eating meals with her, spending all evening with her and then sleeping beneath her roof. She knew she'd feel safe but after the last fiery kiss they had shared, she wondered what else she might feel.

By the time she got out of the shower and re-bandaged her cuts, it was almost eight o'clock and she was utterly exhausted. The adrenaline that had filled her during the attack and immediately afterward was gone.

Instead of putting on regular clothes, she pulled on her nightshirt and then added her robe on top. She didn't have to worry about her hair; it would do its usual thing and dry curly.

She left the bedroom and found Sam sitting on the edge of the sofa. No smile greeted her and he appeared unusually somber.

"We need to talk," he said and patted the space next to him.

She sank down, her heart once again beating an unnatural rhythm. Maybe he had made the offer to stay here with her in the heat of the moment and now that he'd had a few minutes to think about it, he'd changed his mind.

He reached out and took her hands in his. "Harper, I believe the person who is after you is angry because we're dating. First it was the doll and the note, and then the attack on you. Being around me is obviously dangerous for you. Even though this is the last thing I want to do, maybe it would be best if I distance myself from you."

"No." The word snapped out of her. She drew in a deep breath and squeezed his hands as her mind reeled with his words. "Sam, if you want to distance yourself from me because you don't want to see me anymore, that's one thing. But I absolutely refuse to let some lunatic dictate who I have and who I don't have in my life. I won't lie, I'm frightened, but this just makes me so angry."

"I'll tell you one thing, I definitely don't want to stop seeing you. But it pains me to think that I'm the reason you're in danger," he replied.

"Sam, what if we quit seeing each other and I start dating another man that this creep doesn't like? Will I be terrorized all over again? Will he try to kill me again? Don't you see? I can't give him that much power over me. And the last thing I want to do is stop seeing you. So, it's settled, we're still dating."

"If that's a risk you're willing to take, then I'm all in." He smiled at her, that wonderful smile that lit her up inside and now made her feel safe.

"Besides, we can't know for sure that you're the reason this man came after me," she said.

"After the note and the doll you received, it's an educated guess that I'm your problem," he replied, the somber look once again on his features. "And I don't want us to fool ourselves about that."

"It doesn't matter. As far as I'm concerned, it's settled. I'm not letting anyone push you out of my life. You leave my life when you want to, not when somebody else wants you to. And now, I'm ready for bed. I'm completely exhausted," she said. "Let me show you to my spare bedroom."

They both got up from the sofa and she led him down the hallway and into the second bedroom. Thankfully she felt the bedroom was a nice one, with a queen-size bed covered in a navy spread. There was a long dresser and a chest of drawers, most of which were empty and ready for use.

"You're welcome to stay up as late as you want and the sound of the television won't bother me at all," she said. "The sheets on the bed are clean and there are clean towels in the hall bathroom linen closet."

"Thanks, I'll be just fine," he replied. "After everything that's happened, I hope you get a good night's sleep." He leaned forward and gave her a gentle kiss on her forehead. "And don't worry, I'm on duty here and nobody is going to get past me to get to you, and that's a promise."

"Thanks, Sam, and now I'll just say good-night." She left his bedroom and went into hers across the hall.

Taking off her robe, she then turned out the lights and got into bed. The wind outside had apparently chased all the clouds from the sky, for a bright beam of moonlight drifted through her window.

She closed her eyes, but almost immediately her head filled with visions of her attacker. His eyes had appeared so dark and so filled with hate. She could smell his rage toward her, feel his body heat threatening to consume her. In her mind's eye she saw the knife coming toward her again and again. Her body tensed in fight-or-flight mode even as she told herself she was safe and sound.

Taking deep breaths in and out, she tried to relax, but residual fear continued to grip her, tightening her chest. Now that Sam's truck was parked out front, surely her attacker wouldn't try to break into the house. Sam was on duty now and she was perfectly safe, she reminded herself.

But realistically, how long could Sam stay here with her? How long might it take Dallas to identify and arrest the person? Realistically, it could take weeks...even months. Heck, Dallas might never catch the person who had attacked her.

A tree branch danced at her window, not an uncommon occurrence, but tonight it shot her straight up in bed, her heart beating a million miles a minute.

Despite how tired she was, she was never going to get to sleep. She was still too afraid and that fear made her heartbeat race with anxiety. She was afraid to be alone in the dark and in her own bed.

She tried...she really tried, but after another agonizing few minutes had passed with her being unable to relax, she slid out of bed. She had no idea what door she might be opening, but once she'd made up her mind, she refused to reconsider her actions. She was afraid and she knew the only way she could sleep at all tonight was if Sam was by her side in her bed.

The house was quiet and dark, indicating to her that Sam had gone to bed as well. His door was open and she moved to stand in the threshold. "Harper?" He immediately sat up, obviously seeing her in the moonlight.

"Sam...could you...uh... Could you maybe come sleep with me? I... I'm still a little afraid." She was shocked by how badly her voice trembled.

"Of course," he said without any hesitation. He

got out of bed. He was clad only in a pair of dark boxers and in the moonlight she couldn't help but admire his half-naked body. His shoulders were so wide and his hips were slim. His broad chest gleamed in the silvery light that danced through the window. All she could think about was how safe she would feel with him next to her.

"I don't mean to be a baby," she said.

"I don't think you're a baby," he replied. "You're a woman who went through a terrifying ordeal."

When he reached her in the hallway, he took her hand with his and allowed her to lead him into her bedroom. Once there she got back into bed and he crawled in on the other side. "Better?" he asked softly.

"Uh…could…could you maybe hold me for a few minutes, maybe just until I fall asleep?" she asked tentatively. It was embarrassing how needy she felt in this moment.

In silent reply he reached out and drew her into his arms and against his body. Feeling his warmth surrounding her, his strength protecting her, she sighed and finally relaxed into him.

"Better now?" he repeated.

"Definitely much better," she replied softly.

She could hear his heartbeat. Strong and steady, it didn't sound like the beat of impending sleep. She also found that his closeness had chased away any desire she had for sleep. Instead, she found herself desiring something else.

Sam.

"Are you sleeping?" she asked softly, even though she knew he wasn't.

"Not yet…why?"

"I can't sleep," she replied.

"Do you want to get up and talk for a little while?" he asked. "Or maybe would you like to go sit on the sofa and watch some television to try to make you sleepy?"

"Not really."

"Harper, what can I do to help you?" he asked.

She hesitated only a moment. "I want you to kiss me, Sam. I… I want you to make love to me." Had she really said that out loud? She felt him tense against her. "I'm sorry, Sam. Forget I said it, forget I said anything," she said hurriedly.

"Harper, why on earth would I want to forget it? I'd love to make love to you, but I don't want to just because you're afraid or you can't sleep. I need to know you really want me as much as I want you."

He wanted her? Just knowing that shot a new, hot desire through her veins. "I want you, Sam. I wanted you the last time we kissed. And oh, I so want you now."

She barely got the words out of her mouth before his lips took hers in a fiery kiss that half stole her breath away. Their tongues danced wildly together as he pulled her closer and closer yet against him.

His hands stroked up and down her back…so

warm she could feel his heat through the cotton
of her nightshirt. Her entire body warmed and she
suddenly wondered if she was having a hot flash.

Oh Lordy, not now, she mentally protested. The
very last thing she wanted was for him to see her
face and chest turn beet red. The very last thing
she wanted to do was break out in a sweat in his
arms because of the hormonal mayhem that was
occasionally her personal glimpse into hell.

She started to pull back from him and then she
realized the warmth inside of her was not a hot
flash at all. Rather it was the delicious, Sam-in-
spired flames of desire.

Now that she recognized what it was, she
wanted more. She wanted so much more. She hun-
gered for his touch everywhere on her body. She
wanted to be naked with him. With that thought in
mind, she completely leaned back from him and
drew her nightshirt over her head and tossed it to
the side just off the bed.

This was the real moment of truth. Her breasts
were not as perky as they'd once been and there
was no place to hide her tummy pouch. She knew
she was completely visible to him in the moon-
beams that crept into the window.

She placed one arm across her breasts and the
other one across her stomach. Sam, on the other
hand, looked positively gorgeous with his broad,
tanned chest and strong upper arms.

"Harper," he said gently. "Please don't try to

hide yourself from me." He took the arm that covered her breasts and moved it aside. "You have no reason to hide. You are positively beautiful."

It wasn't his words that made her feel so desirable, rather it was the gleam in his eyes…a hungry glint that made her believe what he said. Suddenly she felt beautiful and desirable and it was a wonderful feeling she hadn't felt in years and years.

He pulled her back into his arms and this time as they kissed, she had the intense pleasure of feeling his naked, warm skin against her own. It felt utterly amazing.

He then shifted her to the side of him and he leaned over her. His mouth slid from her lips to kiss slowly down her jawline and then down onto the length of her throat.

Shivers of pleasure swept over her. She couldn't remember having this wild desire, this crazy hunger for a man ever before in her entire life.

When his tongue flicked across the tip of one of her breasts, a breathless gasp escaped her. Electric currents shot from her breasts to the very center of her being. He sucked and licked, driving her half-mad with pleasure.

"Sam." His name escaped her without her volition.

He raised his head, his eyes glittering like a primal being's. "Do you want me to stop? I'll stop anytime you want, Harper. You're in charge here."

"No…don't stop. Please don't stop," she replied hungrily.

His white teeth flashed as he grinned and then he returned to lavishing her breasts with his tongue. His other hand caressed down the length of her side and then her hip.

Every muscle in her body tensed in sweet anticipation. There were no more thoughts of the attack, or the pain of any of the slash wounds. There was only Sam…sweet, sweet Sam.

His hand reached the edge of her panties. "Sweet Harper," he said, his words mirroring her thoughts. She wished she was wearing hot-pink or sexy black silk underwear. She wished she had on a racy, wispy kind of underpants. Instead, she had on a pair of plain white cotton panties.

It didn't seem to matter as he hung a thumb into the waistband and slowly pulled them down. She arched her hips to allow him to drag them completely off her, then she kicked them to the side.

Her desire for him spiraled even higher. He swirled his fingertips across the sensitive skin of her inner thigh, making her want…need him to touch her even more intimately. She was on fire and when he did finally touch her moist center, she nearly burst into flames.

His fingers moved against her slowly, softly at first and then he picked up the rhythm and pressure as the tension inside her climbed higher and higher.

Then she was there, shuddering and crying out his name as she rode a tidal wave of release that left her utterly boneless. Still, she wanted more… she now wanted him to possess her completely, but as he moved to do just that, she shoved him onto his back.

She now wanted to pleasure him. She wanted to tease and torment him until he could stand it no longer. She wanted to be the best lover he'd ever had…ever would have.

He stared up at her and she leaned over him and kissed him with all her heart, with all her soul. Their tongues once again swirled together in a heated dance. When the kiss finally ended, she slid her hands down and across his chest, then nipped and kissed the warm, firm skin.

His breathing came hard and fast, as did hers as she reached the edge of his black boxers. She began to pull them down, but he stopped her. "You have to stop," he said with a groan. "If you don't stop now, I'll be finished before we get started." He gently pushed her back to his side.

He then kicked off his boxers and moved between her thighs. She welcomed him, grabbing him by his buttocks and urging him forward.

He eased into her and then froze. "Oh, Harper, you feel so good." His voice was a low growl of pleasure.

"Oh, so do you," she moaned. He filled her up completely. Then he began to thrust into her. In and out, slowly…steadily he built a new rising tension inside her. All she could think about was Sam and this moment.

Soon, they moved together faster, more frantically, and their breaths became pants and moans. She moaned his name again and again as the pressure inside her grew in intensity. Then she was there again, exploding into a million pieces as he also found his release.

When it was all over, he leaned down and kissed her. It was a soft, gentle kiss that reached in to caress her very soul. "Are you okay?" he asked.

She smiled up at him. "I'm better than okay. What about you?"

He chuckled. "I am way, way better than okay." He rolled away from her and slid out of the bed. "I'll be right back."

She got up as well. She grabbed her nightgown and panties and then headed for her en suite bathroom. The fear that had driven her to invite Sam into her bedroom was momentarily gone. It had been replaced by the warmth of their lovemaking.

It had been wonderful to feel the strength of a man's arms around her again, to feel his desire for her in every move he'd made. She'd forgotten the utter and complete joy of sharing passion. But she knew the real joyfulness of it had come because it had been Sam. She wanted…needed Sam and nobody else.

Their connection hadn't just felt like a physical

one. It had been the connection of heart and soul and she felt closer to Sam than she'd ever felt with anyone before in her entire life.

She quickly pulled her nightgown back over her head and for several long moments she stared at her reflection in the mirror as a sudden, horrible thought lodged in her mind. She had sworn it would never happen. It was definitely something she hadn't wanted to happen, but it had.

She was nothing but a fool, for she had fallen crazy and madly in love with Sam Bravano.

He paced back and forth in his living room, a rich anger ripping through him. He'd tried his best to kill her tonight. It had been perfect. He'd managed to disable her car and then he had followed her to her front door. Everything had been so perfect, but somehow the bitch had managed to survive his attack.

As he thought of her with the much younger Sam, it completely sickened and disgusted him. And it made him think of his wife, Bettina. After twelve years of marriage that bitch had been going to leave him for a much younger man. In fact, she'd crowed about it, telling him her young lover had more stamina in the sheets than he ever would.

He'd been a good husband to her. He'd spent all the years of his marriage trying to make her happy. He'd worked hard and had been financially generous toward her. He'd made sure she had almost everything she wanted within reason.

He'd known she'd been cheating on him, but he'd figured it was just a fleeting thing and when her affair fell apart, he would forgive her. Until that night, when she'd thrown it all up in his face and had her bags packed and ready to leave.

He hadn't meant to hit her as hard as he had. He really hadn't meant to hit her at all. It had just happened. He'd been so damned angry with her and she'd been so cruel. He'd hit her with an uppercut that had snapped her head backward. Then she had fallen and hit her head on the side of the coffee table. He definitely hadn't meant for her to die, but she had.

Crack. He still remembered the sound her head had made when it hit the wooden surface. For him, it had been the sound of justice. After that everyone in town had thought she'd packed her bags and left him. The truth was, he kept her very close to him now.

Harper had sparked something inside him and he was just waiting and working up his nerve to ask her out. He'd finally decided he was ready for a new relationship with her.

When he heard about her dating the much younger Sam, old memories had shot through his head, bad memories of his wife and her young lover.

He was bitterly disappointed in Harper but more

than that she'd stirred an enormous rage inside him that had made him decide she needed to die. She needed to be punished just like Bettina had been punished.

He'd warned her first with the doll and the note. She should have taken that warning and stopped seeing the young man. But she hadn't. And tonight, his rage toward her had been all-consuming, but he'd failed to punish her the way she really needed to be punished.

He finally stopped pacing and sank down on his sofa. Oh well, tomorrow was another day. One way or another he'd make Harper pay for her sin. And the payment was death.

Chapter 8

Sam awoke with the sound of Harper's alarm clock ringing. It was four-thirty in the morning, the world was still dark and he was spooned closely around her body.

"Hmm, I hate to get up," she whispered sleepily.

He hated to leave the bed, too. She was so soft, so warm against him, and thinking about what they had shared the night before fired a new desire for her. She'd been a wonderful lover, so giving and passionate, and he'd not only been stirred by their lovemaking but also their emotional connection.

"Take the day off," he suggested. "Lord knows you've earned it, especially after last night. You could take the day to rest and relax and go back to work when you feel ready."

"Hmm, I could, but I won't. I've got a ten-year-old little girl having a birthday party today and her mother is going to pick up three dozen cupcakes for the event. I can't let them down."

Reluctantly, he rolled away from her and got out of bed. "Okay then, come on, woman. If you insist that you're going to work today, then it's time for you to get up and go bake." He turned on the bedside lamp.

She rolled over and smiled at him. She looked utterly charming with her hair wild and curly and her beautiful blue eyes shining so brightly. "What kind of cookies do you want me to bake for you today?"

"You know I'm partial to your oatmeal raisin ones."

"Then oatmeal raisin it is." She got out of bed and stretched with her arms overhead, exposing not only the tops of her shapely legs, but also a hint of her sexy derriere. Her body excited him. He loved that she wasn't a skinny little thing, but rather she had a little meat on her bones. She had a mature kind of body and he positively loved it.

They parted ways to go shower and dress, him in the hall bathroom and her in her own bathroom. Twenty minutes later they were ready to leave the house.

He drove her to the bakery and came inside with her. It was too early for him to begin working outside so he sat in the folding chair in the kitchen and watched her as she went about her morning routine.

"I think I'll do a batch of brownies for today," she now said. "It's been a minute since I've baked them and they are always a favorite among the customers."

"Brownies always sound good to me," he replied.

So far, the morning conversation had all been business related, but he now decided it was time to talk about more personal things.

"Should we talk about last night?" he asked.

She looked at him in surprise. "Do we need to?"

"I don't know, everything moved pretty quickly and I was wondering if you had any regrets," he replied.

She gazed at him for a long moment and then shook her head. "No regrets here. What about you?" A dainty frown creased the center of her forehead and she seemed to be holding her breath.

He smiled at her. "Definitely no regrets here, but we didn't even talk about birth control. We definitely weren't thinking about that last night."

"I'm on the pill and I haven't been with anyone since I was married." A faint blush danced into her cheeks.

"And I haven't been with anyone in over a year and I'm clean." He offered her another smile. "Thankfully we got all of that out of the way."

"Really?" She looked at him skeptically.

"Really what?" He eyed her curiously.

"You haven't…uh…been with anyone for over a year?" Once again that charming blush filled her cheeks and she averted her gaze from his. "I find that a little hard to believe."

"Well, believe it. Harper, it's the honest-to-God truth. I decided about a year ago that I'd rather be celibate for a while than have empty, meaningless sex with some random woman." He was being perfectly honest with her. He'd had enough meaningless sex in his early to late twenties to last a lifetime. "I smell cookies."

"My cookies!" She whirled around to the oven and withdrew a large baking pan of the golden-brown treats. She placed the pan on a cooling rack and then turned back to him, her hands on her hips. "You are definitely a big distraction in my kitchen, Sam Bravano."

He laughed. "I'm not trying to be. Do you want me to go sit at a table in the other room?"

"Absolutely not," she replied with a laugh of her own.

It felt good. The kitchen was warm and smelled like a touch of heaven with all the things she was baking.

It also felt oddly intimate with just the two of them here while other people were still in their beds and the sun had yet to rise. In the kitchen with Harper was a nice place to be.

He started asking her questions, interested

in what all she was mixing up and baking. He watched in admiration as she expertly frosted three dozen cupcakes with bright pink frosting and tiny flowers in white. She then moved on to decorate three different kinds of cakes.

It was obvious she loved what she did and she moved from one task to the next with a graceful efficiency that he admired. The conversation was easy between them and the time seemed to fly. Suddenly the sun was up and after helping her carry some of the goodies from the kitchen and into the display case, he left her to head outside.

He glanced over to the tattoo shop, which wasn't open yet for the day. When RJ came in, Sam definitely intended to have a little chat with the man. He hadn't forgotten that yesterday RJ had come into the bakery to complain about something he had no right to complain about.

In the meantime, he had work to do. As he got busy, he tried to keep his mind off the fact that somebody had attacked Harper with deadly intent the night before.

If he dwelled on it for too long, he'd be so angry he wouldn't be able to be what he felt she needed right now. What he thought she needed from him now was his calm and steadiness. She needed his light tone and perhaps a little more flirtation to keep her mind off the fear he knew she had to be feeling.

Even though she hadn't spoken of the attack this

morning, he'd seen the shadows that occasionally darkened her eyes, shadows that made him want to kill somebody.

He hoped like hell Dallas and his men had found something to help them identify the bastard that was responsible for the attack. He wanted the man who had caused the fear, the pain and the dark shadows in her eyes to be thrown in jail for a very long time.

The bakery officially opened for the day and some of the regulars began to show up. "Hey, Sam," Mark Lindey greeted as he approached the front door.

"Hi, Mark. How you doing?" Sam replied. Mark was in his mid-fifties and owned a small farm on the outskirts of town. He was a divorced man who often stopped in at the bakery for an hour or so in the mornings.

"I'm doing okay," Mark replied. "Eventually I need to talk to you about some work that needs to be done on my front porch. It's rotting and starting to fall apart. It definitely needs to all be replaced."

"Just give me a call whenever you're ready to get the work done," Sam replied.

"It will probably be late fall before I'm ready to get it going," Mark said.

"I'm sure that will work for us. We'll be around whenever."

"Now I'm heading inside to have coffee with

my favorite woman, who makes the best cinnamon rolls I've ever eaten in my life."

Sam laughed. "She does make a mean cinnamon roll."

It was just before ten o'clock when Sam saw RJ approaching his shop. He put his hammer down and strode over to the big man. "Hey, RJ," he said as he got closer to the tatted man. "You got a problem with me?"

RJ narrowed his eyes. "I was just wondering how long this crap is going to be out here," he said and gestured toward the supplies stacked to the side of the bakery entrance.

"As long as it takes," Sam replied. The muscle-bound, tattooed bully certainly didn't scare Sam. "My supplies aren't bothering your business and there's no reason to take any complaints you have to Harper. You got a problem with something you bring it to me, but you leave her the hell alone."

"What are you? Her bodyguard?" RJ said sarcastically.

"Actually, right now I am," Sam replied. "She was attacked last night. Somebody tried to kill her…to stab her to death. So, where were you last night?"

"Whoa." RJ took a step backward. "I don't know anything about an attack. I had nothing to do with whatever happened to Harper last night. Don't try to pin anything like that on me."

"I won't, but I'm sure you'll be hearing from

Dallas at some point, especially considering your harassment of Harper yesterday just before she was attacked." Sam didn't wait for a reply. Instead, he turned around and headed back to the bakery.

He didn't really believe RJ was the guilty party. RJ might be many things, including a bully, but Sam couldn't see him actually attacking a woman. Despite RJ's bad boy looks and big attitude, Sam had never heard of the man having any issues with the law.

He got back to work and around one, when the traffic in the bakery was in a lull, he knocked off and went inside. She greeted him with the smile that always lit a warmth deep inside him.

"Hey, cutie," he said as he walked up to the counter.

"Nobody has ever called me cutie before," she said with a laugh.

"Then you've been running around with the wrong crowd," he replied with a grin. "You are definitely a cutie as far as I'm concerned."

She laughed again and covered her cheeks with her hands. "Somehow you always make me blush."

"I love your blushes," he replied and then laughed as her blush deepened.

"So, what can I do for you?"

"Do you really want me to answer that question?" He raked his gaze down the length of her and then leered at her.

"You are a very bad boy," she said. "Let me rephrase my question… what would you like from the display counter today?"

"I'll just take the usual," he said.

The usual was a cup of coffee and three of her oatmeal raisin cookies. "Take a break with me?"

"Of course," she replied.

He took a seat at one of the tables and a moment later she joined him there with his order. "How are you doing today?" he asked.

"I'm doing fine. I called the garage about my car and somebody is supposed to come out this afternoon to replace the battery."

"That's good, but you won't need to be driving around alone until Dallas gets the person who attacked you last night under arrest."

Her eyes darkened. "I hope that's sooner rather than later."

"Why? Are you tired of my company already?" he said teasingly.

"You know it's not that," she protested.

He reached out and covered her hand with his. "I hope Dallas catches the man sooner rather than later, too." He pulled his hand from hers. "On another note, I had a little chat with RJ earlier. I don't think he'll be bothering you anymore."

"You didn't beat him up, did you?"

He laughed. "Did you want me to beat him up?"

"Maybe just a little," she replied with a naughty grin that absolutely delighted him.

They continued to visit until his cookies were

gone and it was time for Sam to get back to work outside. At five thirty, they left the bakery and agreed to order pizza for dinner.

An hour later they sat at her kitchen table sharing a pepperoni pizza and talking about the events of the day. Sam tried to keep the conversation light and breezy, although the afternoon had revealed something that Sam was keeping to himself.

At the time the mechanic had showed up, there were several people inside the bakery and Sam had offered to take care of the car issue with the mechanic for her.

The minute they opened the hood, Sam saw what the problem was…the battery cables had been intentionally disconnected. Sam's blood had run cold at the discovery.

So, it wasn't by accident that Harper had had to walk home from work the night before. The potential murderer had made sure of it. So the attack had definitely been completely premeditated.

He'd immediately called Dallas with the information, but he hadn't told Harper. All he'd said to her was that one of the battery cables was loose and just needed a quick tightening. He considered it a tiny white lie to protect her.

As he now looked at her across the table, her eyes were sparkling as she picked the pepperoni slices off the pizza and then popped them into her mouth.

She'd been through enough without knowing

about the car. He not only wanted to protect her physically, but emotionally as well. She'd been so strong through all of this.

She'd been attacked the night before and yet hadn't hesitated in going to work this morning because she needed to bake cupcakes for a little girl's birthday party. Many other women would have taken off work for days or perhaps weeks in order to heal from such a horrible experience, but not Harper.

The plan was after they finished eating, they'd go to his house so he could pack up some things to bring back here. One of the main things he wanted to get was his gun.

They were almost finished with their dinner when she suddenly jumped up from the sofa. "Excuse me," she exclaimed and raced for the hall bathroom.

He frowned. What had just happened? Had she suddenly gotten sick? He didn't feel sick and he had eaten the same pizza she had. After a couple of minutes had passed, he got up and knocked on the bathroom door.

"Harper? Are you okay?" he asked worriedly.

"I'm fine." After another minute or so she opened the door and stepped into the hallway. He could tell that she'd wiped down her face. The edges of her hair were damp and her face was slightly flushed.

"Are you sick?" he asked with concern.

"No, I'm fine," she replied and swept past him.

"You obviously aren't fine," he countered and followed her back into the living room. "Was it the pizza? Did it make you sick?"

She whirled around. "Just leave it alone, Sam. I said I was fine," she snapped and then walked over to grab the pizza box on the coffee table.

There was no question he was surprised by her sharp tone. He'd never heard that kind of a tone from her before. She froze for a moment and then set the pizza box back down and turned to gaze at him.

"I'm sorry, Sam. I didn't mean to bark at you. I was just…just embarrassed."

He frowned at her as an uneasiness swept through him. "Uh…embarrassed about what?" What was going on with her?

"I was embarrassed to tell you that I…uh, had a hot flash." She averted her gaze from him and it was obvious she was mortified.

He relaxed. He knew all about hot flashes from his mother. Years ago, she would often sit in a kitchen chair and fan herself with a hand towel while cursing at her body.

"Hey, there's absolutely nothing for you to be embarrassed about," he said. He reached out and drew her into his arms. He grinned down at her. "All I care about is that I'm the only man giving you hot flashes."

She smiled up at him in obvious relief. "I can

promise you that, and thank you for being understanding."

He gave her a quick kiss on her forehead and then released her. "Now, let's get the leftover pizza taken care of so we can head to my place and I'll pack up some things to bring back here."

"Sounds like a plan," she replied. "And thanks again, Sam."

As they left her house to go to his, he couldn't help but think about how much he cared about her. He definitely wanted to see where the two of them were going with their relationship, but he had to keep her alive in order to do that.

Sunday late morning Harper stood in front of her bathroom mirror, her heart beating a little faster than usual. Sam had told her to dress casually for the day so she was clad in a blue sleeveless blouse and a pair of white capris. Her makeup was light and with a final glance in the mirror, she turned and left the bathroom.

Sam had just finished showering and was still in the second bedroom getting dressed. She went into the kitchen to retrieve the chocolate fudge cake she had baked to take with them and then she sat on the sofa to wait for him.

After they'd finished their pizza and after her hot flash a couple of nights before, they had gone to his house so he could pack up some clothing and personal items to take back to her place.

She had been mortified about the hot flash. She hadn't wanted him to see it happening and so she'd raced for the bathroom to hide. Once she'd admitted to him what had happened, he'd been so sweet about it he'd instantly put her at ease. He was such an amazing guy.

The hot flashes were a part of her life right now and she was glad she had told him about them. It would have been awkward constantly trying to hide them from him while he was living with her.

Once they had gotten to his place, she'd been impressed not only by the house itself, but by all the work he had already accomplished inside to update things.

The upstairs rooms had all been repainted in a soft, buttery beige and the oak wood floors had been refinished and shone with a glossy beauty.

They'd talked about what would be nice for kitchen flooring and then he had gone upstairs to gather his things while she sat to wait on the sofa in the living room.

For just a few minutes as the two of them had talked about the pros and cons of different flooring, it had felt like they were a married couple discussing it. It had been a crazy fantasy that she couldn't let into her head. They were not and would never be a married couple.

And now she was going to meet his family. Another wave of nerves jangled through her. Would they like her? Sam had told her over and over again that they would all love her, but she couldn't help the doubts that flew through her head.

Would his mother like her or would she have a problem with her handsome, hunky son dating an older woman? What about his brothers? And his sister? What would Harper be walking into? Would it be a hostile crowd?

Sam had slept in her bed since the night of the attack and they had made love another time. It had been just as wonderful as the first time. He had definitely gotten into her heart and yet there was a little part of herself that she held back, knowing that eventually they would part ways.

And they would part ways. There was no way their relationship would last forever. Eventually Sam would tire of her and she needed to remind herself of that fact all the time. She couldn't allow herself to completely buy into the fantasy that they would be together forever. She would never be enough for Sam long-term.

At that moment Sam came into the room. As always, her breath caught in her chest at his bold handsomeness. Clad in a pair of black jeans and a white polo that showcased his strong biceps and broad shoulders, he looked as hot and hunky as ever.

"You look very pretty," he said to her with that special smile he had.

"Thank you. You look nice, too."

"Are you ready to go?" he asked.

"As ready as I can get." She stood and grabbed the cake. It would be around eleven when they got to his mother's house and the meal wasn't planned until after noon. She would have at least an hour or so just to visit with his family.

"Are you nervous?" he asked once they were in his truck and heading down the street.

"I'm absolutely terrified," she admitted.

He laughed and reached out to briefly touch the back of her hand. "Don't be. I've told you before, they're all going to love you, and I hope you love them, too."

"I hope you're right," she replied. They might like her as a person, but would they really like her as an older woman dating Sam?

"You're going to love the meal. I might be partial, but my mom makes the best Italian dishes you'll ever taste." He turned the steering wheel to make a left turn.

"I already got a taste of her cooking when you brought me dinner, and it was absolutely delicious," she replied. With each block that passed the knot of nerves in the pit of her stomach tightened.

"I'll tell you one thing, Mom is going to love that cake. Chocolate cake has always been her favorite kind of dessert."

"I hope she enjoys it," Harper replied.

"Trust me, she will, and it looks absolutely beautiful. Those pink flowers on top really look nice against the chocolate frosting."

"Thanks," she replied. She'd taken special care in the decoration, wanting to make the cake not only delicious but also a treat for the eyes. She was pleased with the way it had turned out.

He finally pulled into the driveway of a large attractive two-story house with forest green shutters and a matching front door. There was a huge wraparound porch with a swing and several outdoor chairs, giving an air of warmth and welcome.

There were several other vehicles parked in the driveway. She assumed they belonged to Sam's siblings and once again anxiety flooded her veins and tightened her chest.

"So, this is your childhood home," she asked when he shut off the engine of his truck.

"This is it."

"It's very nice," she replied.

"Thanks. I had a really good childhood here. This house holds a lot of good memories." He got out of the truck and came around to open her door. He took the cake from her so she could get out and then together they walked up to the front door.

He didn't knock, but instead ushered her into the house. They walked into an entryway with an attractive wooden coatrack bench. On the right was a small formal living room holding a beautiful antique-looking sofa and matching chairs in gold fabric.

Sam led her forward and into a great room where two young men were sprawled on an overstuffed gray sofa. They both stood as Sam introduced them as his brothers, Michael and Tony.

Pleasantries were exchanged and then Sam took her through a large archway and into a huge kitchen. It was decorated with a Mediterranean flair and a huge wooden table ruled the space in front of four floor-to-ceiling windows. The table was already set with bright yellow and red plates.

Sam's mother, Antoinette, was a short, slightly round dark-haired woman with lively brown eyes and a beautiful smile. Sam had obviously gotten his great smile from his mother. She greeted Harper with a warm hug and then took the cake plate from her. "You shouldn't have done this," she said. "It's gorgeous and it looks delicious."

"Something certainly smells delicious in here," Harper said. "And thank you so much for having me today."

"I needed to meet the woman my son has been raving about," Antoinette replied with another smile. "Now go…out of my kitchen. I'll let you all know when the food is on the table."

"Is there anything I can do to help?" Harper asked.

"Nothing. Go sit, have a glass of wine and relax." Antoinette gave Sam's shoulder a firm shove. "Go."

Sam laughed. "Okay, okay, we're going." He grabbed Harper's hand. "Don't feel bad, Harper. She never lets anyone in her kitchen when she's cooking a big meal."

He led her back to the great room and motioned toward the love seat. "Would you like a glass of wine?" he asked as he went to a small corner bar in the room. "I'm having one," he added as if to put her at ease.

"Okay, then I'll have a small glass," she said. She sank down on the love seat and once again her nerves tightened her chest as she felt Tony and Michael's curious gazes on her.

"I'm surprised you don't want a huge glass of wine if you have to hang around that big lug for any length of time," Tony said and gestured toward Sam. Michael snickered and Sam rolled his eyes.

"Funny man," Sam replied. He carried both glasses of wine across the room. He handed her one and then sank down next to her on the love seat.

"By the way, we were really sorry to hear about the attack on you, Harper. Does Dallas have a suspect in mind?" Michael asked.

"Unfortunately, no," she answered.

"I can tell you this, nobody is ever going to get close enough to hurt her again," Sam said fervently.

"That's our boy," Tony said.

"Seriously, he's staying with you right now?" Michael asked Harper.

"He is. I'm not sure what I'd do without him right now," she replied with a warm glance at Sam.

"How are things with you and Paula?" Sam asked his brother.

Michael smiled. "Things are pretty good with us right now. She would have been here today but she had already planned to spend the day with her mother. We're supposed to get together later this evening."

"I think he needs to break up with her for good," Tony said.

"Nobody asked you for your opinion," Michael retorted.

"Ignore their bickering, Harper," Sam said. "It's a commonplace thing." Sam then looked at Michael. "I'm just glad things are good with you and her right now," Sam replied.

"Yeah, for now," Tony added. "Things could always change between them in the next hour." Tony laughed as Michael glared at him.

"Paula is Michael's girlfriend, but their relationship has been off and on for the last several months," Sam explained to Harper.

"Relationships can be really hard," Harper said with a sympathetic smile at Michael.

"That's for sure," Michael replied. "But we're working on it. I'm really crazy about her."

As the three men began to talk about work and caught up with each other, it was easy to see that the two younger brothers greatly admired Sam, despite their teasing each other back and forth.

More than once Harper found herself laughing

as Tony and Michael told stories about a much younger Sam. Sam's brothers were very friendly with her and slowly Harper's nerves began to disappear.

They had all been talking for about a half an hour when Sam's sister and her husband came in. Lauren was a beautiful woman with long black hair and lively dark eyes. She and her husband, Russ, seemed very nice. Sam made the introductions between them and Harper, and then Russ sat in one of the two armchairs that completed the sitting area, while Lauren headed for the kitchen.

A moment later she came back out with her mother at her side. "Now, what's going on here? I need to get back to my cooking," Antoinette said.

"Ma, I wouldn't have pulled you out of your kitchen if it wasn't important," Lauren replied. "Now, I have a big announcement to make." She paused for a moment, obviously for dramatic effect, and then continued. "Russ and I...we're pregnant."

Antoinette squealed with happiness and threw her arms around her daughter. "Oh, this is what I've been waiting for since you all grew up," she said. "A grandchild for me." She released her daughter and wiped at the tears that had sprung to her eyes.

"Congratulations, Lauren," all her brothers said.

Michael got up and shook Russ's hand. "Good man," he said to his brother-in-law.

"Tell me more," Antoinette said, still wiping happy tears from her eyes. "How far along are you?"

"A little over three months," Lauren replied.

"You kept this secret from me for so long?" Antoinette asked.

"I didn't want to tell anyone until I was this far along," Lauren replied.

"It doesn't matter now. So, am I having a little boy grandbaby or a little girl?" Antoinette asked eagerly.

Lauren laughed. "We don't know yet. We specifically didn't want to know. In the next month or so we'll have a little reveal party."

"You aren't going to shoot off a cannon or get into a hot-air balloon, are you?" Tony asked.

"Yeah, tell us you aren't going to do something wild and crazy just so you can post it on one of your social media accounts," Michael said.

Lauren laughed. "I can promise you none of those things are going to happen. I'm thinking maybe my doctor can let Harper know the sex of the baby and then she can bake either a pink or blue cake covered in chocolate frosting. We wouldn't know the sex until we cut into the cake."

"I can do that," Harper said with a warm smile at Lauren. "In fact, it would be my honor."

"Now I have to get back to my kitchen, but I am so happy," Antoinette said. She practically danced back into the kitchen and Lauren sank down in the chair next to her husband's.

"I hope it's a boy," Michael said to his sister. "I'd love to be the uncle of a little boy I can teach to play football and baseball."

"Hello? What am I in this equation?" Russ said with a laugh.

"We'll let you have the kid until he's out of diapers," Tony said. "And then we'll take over."

"Trust me, Russ is going to be changing a lot of diapers. It's an equal opportunity kind of deal."

Everyone laughed as Russ made a face. It was so nice for Harper to be sharing in this moment with Sam's family. As the men continued to tease both Russ and Lauren, she just sat and enjoyed the laughter that surrounded her.

"I don't know if Sam mentioned it to you or not, but I'm getting ready to open a shop," Lauren leaned over and said to Harper. "It's going to be a dress shop with lots of fun trinkets and jewelry."

Harper nodded. "Yes, Sam told me about your plans. It sounds like it will be a great place to shop."

"I hope all the women in town think so. Any words of advice from one business owner to another?" Lauren asked.

Harper frowned thoughtfully. "Try to work into your budget extra help. It's easy to burn out if you're working the shop eight or ten hours a day, six days a week," Harper said.

"But isn't that what you've been doing at the bakery?" Lauren asked.

"Yes, but I'm finally ready to make a healthy change for myself and hire some part-time help." Harper had been thinking about it for several days and just now realized she was ready to make a change. Did it have something to do with Sam being in her life? Probably.

Sam looked at her in surprise and reached out to grab her hand with his. "I'm thrilled that you're finally going to give yourself a break." She smiled at him warmly.

She then turned back to Lauren. "I would definitely recommend you hire some help now, especially since you're pregnant."

"The good news is I'll be able to bring the baby with me to work every day."

Harper smiled. "That's one of the positive things about being your own boss and making your own rules."

"Come on, my family. The food is on the table," Antoinette's voice rang out from the kitchen.

"Let's go eat," Tony said and jumped up from the sofa.

There were several minutes of controlled chaos as everyone found seats at the table. Steaming dishes filled the center of the tabletop. There was a huge pan of the eggplant parmesan, a stewpot filled with meatballs and a basket of garlic bread.

Even though there was an empty seat at the head

of the table, Antoinette hovered over everyone to make sure they all got served.

"Ma, sit down," Sam said. "I'm sure you've been on your feet since early this morning."

"She has been," Michael said. "She was up and in the kitchen at the crack of dawn. Ma, you know we like it when you sit and eat with us."

"Okay, okay." Antoinette finally sank down in the empty chair. "Now *mangiare*," she said.

"That means eat in Italian," Sam leaned over and said to Harper.

And eat they did. For the next half an hour or so they ate, they talked and they laughed. Harper found herself charmed by the close-knit family. There was not only great food on the table, but there was also an enormous amount of love in the room.

She would love to belong here and to have big dinners with them once a week. She'd never experienced this feeling of close family before, not in her marriage and not when she was growing up as an only child. For her, it was positively magical.

She also felt accepted here. Nobody had said a word that made her feel like she didn't belong. Her nerves had calmed down to nonexistence.

When they were all finished eating, Harper began to help clear the table, but Antoinette shooed her away. "Go, sit and digest and then we'll bring out your beautiful cake."

"Don't even try to argue with her, Harper. She's as stubborn as the day is long," Sam said.

"That is the truth about me," Antoinette agreed with a wide smile. "I am stubborn and I like to do things my own way. Thank you, Harper, for offering to help, but I'd rather you get out of my kitchen."

Sam laughed and took Harper's arm. "Come on, honey. We aren't welcomed in the kitchen."

Sam and Harper had barely sat back down in the love seat when Lauren smiled at her. "Harper, could we have a little chat on the front porch? I'd like to pick your brain some more and I'm sure it would bore the men in the room to death."

"Sure," Harper replied, assuming the young woman wanted to talk more about the ins and outs of running a business. "I'll be right back," she said to Sam and then followed Lauren out the front door.

"At least it's not too hot in the shade to sit for a little while," Lauren said as she sank down in one of the chairs while Harper opted to sit in the double porch swing.

"I didn't want to bore all my brothers and my husband with more store talk," Lauren said.

"I understand completely," Harper said. "And again, congratulations on your pregnancy."

"Thanks. I feel like in the coming months I'm going to have two births...first my store opening and then the baby coming. I'm over the moon about both," Lauren said, her face glowing with her happiness.

For the next fifteen minutes or so, the two women talked about the business of being in business. Harper tried to tell Lauren all the pitfalls to watch out for and Lauren seemed to appreciate any and all advice she could get from Harper.

"You like my brother a lot," Lauren said. It was more of an observation than a question.

"I do," Harper replied. "He's a wonderful, caring and amazing man."

Lauren nodded. "He is, and he seems to like you a lot, too."

"He tells me he does," Harper replied. A touch of warmth filled her cheeks.

Lauren looked off toward the street and then gazed back at Harper once again. "He told us about the attack on you. I'm so sorry that happened to you."

"Thank you. I have to admit it was pretty horrible."

"And I understand he's acting as a sort of bodyguard for you right now."

Harper fought off a sudden shiver as she thought about the man who had tried to kill her. "Yes, he is…thank God. He's staying with me until the man who attacked me is under arrest."

"Does Dallas have any clues about who he is?" Lauren asked.

"Unfortunately, not that I'm aware of, but we're

hoping he'll come up with something very soon."
Once again Harper fought against a shiver.

"I understand the bodyguard part that he's doing
for you, but do you really think it's fair to him for
you to tie him up romantically?" Lauren's eyes
narrowed slightly. "I mean, let's be real here. You
are quite a bit older than him. I'm assuming you
can't have children. Your relationship with him
would deprive him of having kids and becoming
a father in the future."

"He's told me he doesn't want any children,"
Harper replied, more than a little stunned by Lauren's blunt words to her.

Lauren smiled. "Sam is young. He doesn't know
what he wants. He may change his mind about having children six months from now. You seem like a
very nice woman, Harper. If you really care about
Sam at all and have his best interests at heart, then
you should let him go to find somebody more his
own age."

She didn't give Harper time to reply and, in any
case, Harper didn't know what to say. Lauren got
up from her chair. "And now we better get back in
there before the boys think we ran away."

Lauren's words resonated deep inside Harper
as they all enjoyed the cake she'd baked and then
later when they got back to her house.

"That was fun," Sam said once they were settled on her sofa and relaxing. "Did you enjoy it?"

"It was a good time," she replied. "Your brothers were really nice and they're a real hoot and your mother is a doll. Your sister and brother-in-law were very nice, too."

"I could tell they all liked you, too," he said.

Maybe all but one, Harper thought to herself. Sam had no idea what Lauren had said to her on the front porch and Harper didn't intend to share it with him.

Even as they watched a comedy movie on TV, she couldn't get Lauren's words out of her mind. Would she in some way be holding him back from something if she continued to see him?

Was he too young and not in the right head-space to really know what he wanted out of life? He seemed so mature she sometimes forgot about the age difference between them, but now it was all she could think about.

Maybe she needed to distance herself from him a bit. Perhaps she really needed to think about what she was doing with him. Suddenly it didn't feel like just fun and games with Sam anymore. She was in love with him and everything felt far more complicated now.

It was just after eight when she decided to call it a night. She got up from the sofa and turned to look at him. "I'm really exhausted, Sam." She averted her gaze from him. "I'm so tired, I think I'd like to sleep alone tonight." She looked back at him just in time to see the stunned surprise that crossed his features. The look hurt her, but she needed time to think away from him.

He recovered quickly. "Uh…okay. No problem." He smiled at her. "Whatever you need, Harper."

"Then I'll just say good-night," she said.

"I hope you have sweet dreams," he replied.

Minutes later Harper was in bed and staring up at her darkened ceiling. There was no question she was deeply in love with Sam. But was she somehow cheating him from finding what he really wanted, what he really deserved out of life?

Didn't he really deserve a young woman who could give him a family if he wanted? A young woman who wasn't so settled in her ways and wasn't ready for bed at eight o'clock at night? Somebody who didn't suffer from hot flashes?

She released a deep sigh. The trouble with Sam was he was just too young for her. Now all she had to figure out was if she intended to be selfish and keep seeing Sam romantically, or if she loved him enough to let him go.

Chapter 9

Sam slowly rolled the yellow paint onto the front of the bakery. Harper had picked out the paint last night when the two of them had run to the hardware store. It was a cheerful color that would draw people's attention in a good way to the building.

Even though Sam had always enjoyed the fairly mindless act of painting, today his heart was more than a tiny bit troubled. It had been a little over a week since he and Harper had eaten at his mother's place, a little over a week since she'd first gone to bed alone, and since that time she hadn't invited him back into her bed.

He didn't mind so much not sleeping with her, although he definitely missed her warmth and softness against him, and the scent of her surrounding him while he drifted off to sleep. Then there was the fact that he yearned to make love to her again, but if she wasn't into it right now, then he'd give her the time she needed.

What really bothered him was not only the physical distance between them, but the emotional distance he felt from her. That really bothered him. While she smiled at him and talked to him as usual, he sensed some of their real intimacy had vanished. It was as if she was suddenly holding back from him, and he didn't know why or what had happened.

During the evenings while they'd watched television together, he'd asked her several times if something was wrong between them and she'd insisted everything was fine. But he knew in his heart it wasn't. Things had changed. Something was different and he didn't know why.

The good thing was nothing frightening had happened in the past week. There had been no notes and no strange objects left on her doorstep and things had been quiet and peaceful. But that certainly didn't mean the danger was gone. He remained hyper-vigilant when it came to her protection.

He didn't worry about her when she was at work. There was no way he believed anyone would go into the bakery to try to hurt her, especially given the normal traffic that moved in and out of the establishment. But he did worry about her when they were at her house.

He slept with one eye open and unbeknownst to her, he kept his gun in the top dresser drawer she had allowed him to use for some of his clothing. He not only possessed the gun, but he knew how to use it and would definitely use it to save her life if it came to that.

The sun overhead was hot and made for perfect painting weather. The forecast was for the heat and sunshine to continue through the week. He hoped to get the front of the building painted today except for the trim, and then he'd move to the rest of it starting tomorrow. When he had the whole building painted except for the back, he would then trim it all out. True to her desire, the trim would be a hot pink.

He was hoping to get Harper's take on what she wanted in the backyard after she closed up the bakery today. He knew she hadn't been back there since the day Sandy's body had been found, but he was hoping by now she'd be willing to go out there with him by her side.

He was going to be ready to start work on the back within the next week and so it was time for him to learn what she wanted so he could order supplies.

The bakery had been relatively busy during the morning hours as people came in and left with sweet treats in hand. All her regulars had also shown up. He'd seen Joe and Mark and Ranger inside at various times. At around two there was a lull in business and Sam knocked off to take a break.

The cool, air-conditioned air inside was a welcome relief after his hours in the punishing heat. Harper was behind the counter and offered him a brilliant smile as he walked in. "I can't wait to see how the paint looks," she said.

"I think you're going to be very happy with it," he replied, a bit disappointed that her smile wasn't really meant for him, but rather for the paint.

"You want the usual?" she asked.

"Yes, but instead of the coffee, I'll take a glass of iced tea. It's warm out there today." He pulled out his wallet and handed her the money.

"Go sit and I'll bring it to you," she said after handing him his change.

He took a seat at the table closest to the display case. "You really should be eating a proper lunch each day instead of just eating these cookies," she said as she carried the cookies and drink to him.

"I'd much rather have your cookies than a bologna sandwich," he replied. "Besides, there's all kinds of healthy ingredients in these oatmeal raisin treats, right?"

She laughed and sat across from him. "There's also a lot of sugar."

"Which keeps me moving through the afternoons," he replied. He took a bite and then washed it down with the tea. "It looked like you were fairly busy this morning," he said.

"It was nice and steady, which is the way I like it. The day certainly seems to pass more quickly when I have customers inside. Now, tell me how the painting is going outside."

"It's going. I'm hoping to get the front done by closing time today. Then, I was hoping once you close up you and I could go around back and you can tell me exactly what you want out there. That way I can get some measuring done and let you know the estimate for the work out there."

Her eyes darkened and after a long moment she released a heavy sigh. "Okay. I know it's time... past time really. I have to break the ice sometime and I guess today is as good as any day."

"Harper, I'll be right beside you," he said softly.

She smiled, and this time he knew the gesture was meant solely for him. A flutter of warmth shot straight through to his heart. "There you go again, knowing just what I need," she said.

"I try," he replied lightly. But he obviously wasn't succeeding completely. There was no question she'd withdrawn some from him and he didn't know why. All he really knew was that he was desperate to fix it. He didn't know what she needed from him to bring them back to where they'd been with each other a little over a week ago.

"I'm excited to see the new face of Sweet Tooth," she said.

"It's a sunny, bright new face," he replied.

"I'm so happy." Her eyes sparkled brightly and he loved to see her that way. "I've dreamed of this day ever since I bought the building."

They continued talking about the front of the bakery for about another fifteen minutes or so and then Sam returned to his painting. He'd only been working for a few minutes when Dallas pulled in and parked. "Hey, Dallas," Sam greeted as the lawman got out of his car.

"Hi, Sam," Dallas replied. "The paint is looking really good."

"Thanks, it's definitely a better look than what it was before," Sam replied. He put down his paintbrush. "Are you coming with news for us?"

The smile on Dallas's features instantly fell. "Unfortunately, no. I just was in the area and thought I'd check in and see how Harper is doing. Anything I need to know about?"

"Nothing," Sam said. "Thank God, things have been pretty quiet."

"You still staying with her?"

"I am. I don't want that creep to have another chance to harm her," Sam replied.

"I'll just go in and touch base with her," Dallas replied.

"Do yourself a favor and buy some of her cookies. She makes a mean cookie."

Dallas grinned. "I'll do that." He turned from Sam and headed for the front door.

He came back out a few minutes later with a bag in his hand. "Everything looked good in there," he told Sam. "I wound up with cookies, a slice of cake and a big brownie."

Sam laughed. "Tell me about it. I think I've gained five or ten pounds since I started working for Harper."

"Speaking of work, I've got to get back to the office. I'll see you later, Sam."

"See you, Dallas."

Moments later Dallas was gone and Sam was back to painting. He knew Dallas must be stressing hard. He had a potential serial killer at work in the town and the issue of who had tried to kill Harper. Sam couldn't imagine having that kind of pressure every day.

Dallas had already told them that the doll had yielded no fingerprints, nor had the note that had been left with it. Apparently, the creep had been smart enough to wear gloves. It was the same with the clothing she'd worn on the night of her attack. No fingerprints…nothing to help identify the perp. They had also found nothing around her porch area.

It was just before five when he cleaned up the painting supplies and knocked off for the day. He walked into the shop, where Harper was busy with the last-minute things she had to finish up with before closing. "Can you turn the sign for me and get the lights?" she asked.

"Sure." He turned the sign in the door to indicate the bakery was closed and then he flipped the overhead lights off. "Are you ready to head out back?"

"Let me just lock the front door and then I guess I'm ready," she replied. She set aside the cloth she'd been using to wipe down the top of the display case and then she joined him by the front door.

He watched as she locked the door and then he grabbed her free hand in his. "It's going to be all right," he said and gently squeezed her hand.

She released a deep sigh. "I know it will be. It's just the first step out there that I'm dreading," she replied. "I can't help but think about Sandy."

"We'll get through this together," he replied and she cast him a tentative smile.

As they walked past the display counter, she dropped her keys on top and then they headed through the kitchen. Her footsteps slowed when they hit the small laundry room. She ground to a halt just in front of the back door.

She looked up at Sam, her blue eyes dark with anxiety, and a frown cut across her forehead. "Sam, please, could you just take a look out there and make sure nothing is out there that doesn't belong out there?"

He looked out the windowpanes in the door and then smiled at her. "All I see is green grass and some pretty purple and pink flowers you must have planted out there at some point or another."

She released an audible sigh of relief. "Okay, then let's go."

He opened the door and together they stepped outside. He felt her visibly relax and he released her hand. "See, it's okay," he said softly. "Now, show me exactly what you have in mind for back here."

For the next hour or so they talked about the renovations she wanted done. She became more and more animated as she explained to him about the covered porch she envisioned. She wanted it big enough to seat at least eight tables beneath it. It was definitely not just a job for Sam, and he would need his brothers' help in constructing the porch.

He did some quick measurements and wrote them down in his pad and then looked around the backyard area. "Maybe we could put some sort of a pretty fountain or water feature in the center of the yard," he suggested. "You know, a visual point that would make it very peaceful to sit out here."

"Oh, I love that idea," she replied and clapped her hands together. "And then we could plant a lot of flowers around it. In fact, I want a lot of plants and flowers in the yard and all around the porch. I want the area to positively explode with color."

"We can definitely do that," he agreed. "We will make it a beautiful and relaxing place for people to sit and eat whatever you offer for sale."

"I have a lot of plans for the menu," she said, her blue eyes sparkling. God, he loved it when she looked that way. For the past week her eyes hadn't sparkled much.

Once he made sure they were both on the same page, and he'd written everything down, they headed out to go home. Home. He'd definitely come to feel like he was home in her house.

Once again, she grew quiet on the way home and then later as they ate the chicken and vegetables she'd fixed in the Crock-Pot that morning.

After eating and cleaning up, they went into the living room to watch some television. She curled up in the corner of the sofa and once again he felt her distance both physically and emotionally.

He wanted to ask her what had happened, why she was distancing herself from him, but he also wanted to give her the time she needed to work out whatever might be bothering her. And maybe he was a little bit afraid of what her answer might be if he pressed her about what had happened to cause this detachment he felt from her.

Maybe she just wasn't that into him anymore but still wanted him to be here for her protection. Maybe if he wasn't playing bodyguard for her, she'd send him on his way. An arrow of pain stabbed into his heart as he considered this possibility, and it was at that moment he suddenly realized he'd fallen deep and hard and madly in love with the baker lady.

It scared him more than a little bit, these feelings he'd caught for Harper. They were bigger and deeper than anything he'd ever felt for a woman before in his life.

He now gazed over to her. Her attention appeared to be solely focused on the crime drama show that was playing. Even though he wasn't that far away from her, the distance between them felt immense.

His heart swelled with a depth of emotion. He loved her, from the curly dark hair on her head to the pretty pink polish on her toenails and everything in between. Her soft and warm body totally turned him on like nobody had done in a very long time. He couldn't imagine being with or loving anyone else. She was his person. But was he really her person?

He enjoyed her sense of humor and the deep conversations they had shared. She was kind and caring and such a good person. She was everything he had been looking for.

He loved the life he envisioned here with her, a quiet life of snuggling together on the sofa, watching movies and eating popcorn…a life of working hard and then planning vacations to be taken together.

He was way past the point where he needed a woman to entertain him. Besides, Harper entertained him plenty. He was far beyond the years of needing to go drinking with his buddies out at the bars.

He was ready for the lifestyle he'd have here,

with Harper. As much as he wanted to tell her how he felt, he had a feeling she wasn't ready to hear him…at least not yet. In fact, right now he had no idea what she felt about him or if she even wanted him in her life as a romantic partner. And that thought scared the hell out of him.

Harper sat behind the display case and watched outside as Sam and several other men from the lumber yard unloaded all kinds of supplies and wood and stacked it all to the left of her front door. Excitement filled her as the stack of items grew bigger.

She was thrilled that over the past week the building had all been painted yellow with a touch of trim work in bright pink. The front of the bakery now looked a bit whimsical and like one of her decorated cupcakes.

And now, Sam was about to start the work on the back of the building to finish up the rest of her dream for the bakery. Starting in the next couple of days his brothers would be working with him to construct the new covered porch.

She had a feeling he'd intentionally unloaded the lumber in the front of her shop to tick off RJ. She certainly had no problem with that. RJ might hate the new load of lumber outside her building, but there wasn't a damn thing he could do about it.

Sam.

He'd been a quandary in her head and a pain

in her heart for a little over two weeks now. She went to bed alone each night wanting him…needing him and yet denying herself the pleasure of having him with her.

She knew he cared about her. He might have even convinced himself that he was in love with her. She'd felt his gaze on her in the evenings, sensed his desire for her both emotionally and physically.

If he wasn't being her personal bodyguard, she would have asked him to leave long before now, but when she thought about the attack on her, when she thought about being in the house all alone, she was still afraid.

However, she was aware that she couldn't keep him with her forever. It was bad enough that he'd put his life on hold for almost an entire month for her. Who knew if or when Dallas might be able to make an arrest and remove the threat that might still be out there? Dallas might never catch the person who had attacked her.

Still, she loved the sense of safety Sam's presence in the house provided her, but she now thought, even with the threat against her still out there and present, that it was time to send him back to his own life. She'd reached the conclusion after yet another night of soul-searching. She loved him enough to let him go.

She intended to tell him tonight after dinner that he needed to go. Even though it was killing her, she loved him enough to free him so that he could find a relationship with a woman his own age. Lauren had been right, it was selfish of her to want to keep him in a relationship where his future dreams might not be met.

Throughout the afternoon Sam carried some of the lumber from the front to the backyard. She hoped that when she had the talk with him this evening, he wouldn't decide he could no longer do the job for her.

Of course, they had a contract that protected her from him just walking off the job. But she would never force him to work here if he wanted out.

They were two civil adults. Surely they could part ways romantically yet still keep up a healthy working relationship, but that all depended on him. And she had no idea how he was going to react when she told him it was time for them to part ways romantically.

Her heart was positively breaking as she thought of the night to come. She was madly and crazy in love with Sam. She'd never meant for it to happen, but it had. It had been supposed to be just fun and games with him, but at some point along the line, things had gotten serious.

She was going to miss him terribly. She would miss the sound of his laughter and their deep conversations. She would feel the absence of his cheerful, larger-than-life presence in her home.

More than anything she would miss his gentle

touches and the sweet fire in his forest green eyes when they made love. But his future was important to her. More than anything, she wanted him to be happy and she didn't believe his future happiness was with her.

Thoughts of Sam fell away as one of her customers came in to get the cake Harper had baked for her son's fifth birthday. Neither Allie nor Becky had come in to see her since the night of the community meeting, although both had called her several times.

Unfortunately, the calls had been rather stilted and uncomfortable. It both angered and saddened her that her friends had effectively abandoned her because of who she chose to love. She'd never suspected the judgmental side of them and it hurt her deeply. Well, they'd both be happy after tonight.

Everyone would be happy except for Sam and Harper.

At a few minutes before five o'clock she checked to make sure the back door was locked up and then returned to the front to close up the bakery.

Sam waited for her just outside the front door and he gave her one of his beautiful smiles. "Why don't we order pizza tonight so neither of us has to cook?" he suggested as they headed to his truck. Throughout the course of him living with her, they had taken turns preparing the evening meal.

"That sounds great to me," she replied. "You

look exhausted," she added. He looked hot and a fine line of perspiration rode across his forehead.

"I am tired," he admitted. "Carrying some of that lumber from the front to the back today was a bit draining."

"I was wondering if you had it all dropped off out front just to irritate RJ."

He laughed. "I'd like to say I'm a bit evil like that, but the truth of the matter is the lumber truck wouldn't have been able to fit through your gate and the heaviness of the truck would have torn up your yard. Besides, there's still enough left out front to irritate RJ."

She laughed as well, even as a bittersweet pang rushed through her. There would be few moments of shared laughter with him going forward and that broke her heart all over again.

When they got home, he ordered the pizza and then went directly in to shower and she sank down on the sofa to wait for the pizza delivery. It felt good to be off her feet, but a huge ball of anxiety...of dread and sadness began to tighten her chest. She didn't want to do what she intended to do, but she felt like it was the right thing to do for him, and that was what was important.

She decided to wait to have the talk with Sam until after they'd eaten. She jumped up from the sofa and went into the kitchen to get paper plates for the pizza.

She wanted to stay busy doing something...

anything. If she sat and thought about the night to come, then she feared she would start crying and never, ever stop.

She reminded herself that she was doing the right thing for Sam and that was all that was important to her. He came back into the living room, smelling like minty soap and the cologne that had begun to smell like home to her. He was dressed in a clean pair of jeans and a white T-shirt and looked as handsome…as sexy as she'd ever seen him.

Before she could even greet him, the doorbell rang. "Ah, that should be our dinner." He answered the door and then carried the pizza box to the center of the coffee table. "Before I sit, what's the lady's pleasure to drink? Beer? Soda?"

"I think I'd like a beer," she replied. Maybe it would provide her a little liquid courage for the conversation that was going to happen.

"There's nothing better than a cold beer with pizza. I'll be right back." He disappeared into the kitchen and returned a moment later with two beers and a couple of napkins in hand.

He sank down next to her on the sofa and placed the drinks next to the pizza box, which he then opened. "Mmm, looks good. Hand me your plate and I'll give you a couple of pieces that have the most pepperoni on them."

"Ah, a man after my heart," she replied with a forced lightness.

"I know how you do love you some pepperoni,"

he replied with a grin. He handed her plate back to her and then served himself.

For the next few minutes, they ate and talked about the day's events. He explained to her what the next steps were for the back of the building.

As she listened to him all she could think about was the fact that tonight was the last time she'd be sitting next to him eating a meal and listening to his beautiful deep voice. It was the last night for so many things because it was the last night that he would even be in her house.

The ball of anxiety inside her grew bigger and bigger with each minute that passed, as did an immense sadness. Her heart was being ripped in two, not by him, but rather by herself. But as Lauren's words once again played in her head, she reminded herself again that she was doing the right thing for Sam and that was really all that was important.

All too quickly they'd eaten all they wanted of the pizza and the leftovers had been stowed away in the refrigerator. She rejoined him on the sofa and her anxiety was through the roof.

"What do you feel like watching tonight?" he asked as he picked up the remote for the TV. "Are you in the mood for a comedy, or maybe another crime drama?"

"Actually, Sam, we need to have a talk."

He must have heard the seriousness in her tone for he immediately set the remote control down and turned so that he was facing her, a look of deep concern on his features. "What's up?"

A wealth of emotion filled her as she gazed into his beautiful eyes. Oh, this was going to be so hard. "Sam, I've really enjoyed spending time with you. You're a wonderful, caring man."

The frown deepened across his forehead. "Harper, what's going on? What are you doing?"

She drew in a deep breath. "Sam, I'm sorry, but it's time for you to go home. It's been fun, this little fling we've been having, but it's time for each of us to move on." Her words caused her to ache as she spoke them but she wasn't prepared for the look of utter devastation that swept over Sam's features.

"Little fling?" His eyes darkened. "Is that how you see this…us? Harper, this certainly hasn't been a little fling to me." His gaze swept over her face as if searching for answers. "What's really going on here? What about the threat of somebody trying to kill you?"

"You can't play bodyguard for me forever and we both know Dallas isn't going to make an arrest anytime soon. Besides, nothing has happened in the past several weeks. Maybe the creep found somebody else to harass,"

"Or maybe he hasn't done anything else to you because I've been here with you," he countered. "Harper, I don't feel comfortable just leaving you here all alone when I believe the danger is still out there."

His gaze on her was so intense, and not for the first time she felt as if he was trying to probe deep inside her. "I'm sure I'll be just fine."

He slowly shook his head, his gaze still intense. "I don't feel comfortable leaving you at all. Harper, I… I'm in love with you."

She couldn't help the gasp of surprise that escaped her at his words. She hadn't expected them. When she'd envisioned this difficult conversation, words of love from him hadn't entered her mind.

Now tears of joy and of sheer agony burned at her eyes. Under any other circumstances his profession of love for her would have been exactly what she wanted to hear. Knowing she loved him back but still intended to send him away positively broke her heart.

"Sam, I really think it would be best if you go home now and we start seeing other people." Oh, God, she hoped he would just get up off the sofa and start packing his things. The very last thing she wanted was for this to be a prolonged goodbye.

Chapter 10

Sam's heart thundered in an uneven rhythm as he stared at the woman he loved more than life itself. Harper…her name resounded in his head. He'd somehow felt this coming for the past couple of weeks, ever since she'd distanced herself from him. But he had sworn to himself he wasn't going to lose Harper without a fight, and now was the time to fight.

"Did you hear what I just said to you, Harper? I'm in love with you. I don't want to date anyone else. I love you more than any other woman I've ever loved in my life." He leaned toward her, wanting to touch her, to pull her into his arms, but he was afraid to. "Harper, I want to wake up each morning with you in my arms and I want to fall asleep each night spooned around you."

She closed her eyes, as if his words were too painful to hear. "What happened to change things?" he asked softly. "Please tell me. Make me understand. I thought we were both on the same page, I thought you cared about me as much as I care about you." He edged an inch closer to her on the sofa. She was positively breaking his heart right now.

Her eyes opened, blue misty orbs that gazed at him in what appeared to be abject misery. "Sam, it doesn't matter what I feel. What I need you to know is that we had our time together, I've enjoyed it very much and now it's over."

Over? It couldn't be over. He didn't want it to be over. He moved another inch closer to her, so close he could smell the scent of her, feel her body heat radiating toward him. "Harper, don't you realize that you're contradicting yourself? Of course, it does matter how you feel. And I think if you look deep in your heart, you'll realize you love me, too." His heart thundered in his chest with a horrible dread.

"Please, Sam. Don't make this more difficult than it already is," she said softly.

"Maybe it's difficult because you really don't want to do what you're doing right now," he replied. He reached out for her hand, but she jerked hers back, as if afraid of his touch. "Don't you realize we belong together?" he continued. "Just tell me why you are breaking things off with me. Harper, make me understand what's really going on."

Once again, she closed her eyes. This time when she reopened them there was a hard glint there that he'd never seen before. "It's over, Sam. That's all you need to understand and I want you out of my house tonight." She stood from the sofa. "I'll just be in my bedroom. Please let me know when you're leaving so I can lock up after you."

She was gone from the room before he even had a chance to respond. He heard the sound of her bedroom door shutting, the heartbreaking sound of finality.

For a long moment he couldn't move. His mind refused to believe what had just happened, but his heart hurt more than it had ever pained him in his entire life. Was this really it? No real explanations, no real answers as to what was really going on with her. No glimpse into her mind to give him any clue as to what had prompted this sudden decision.

Did she really not care about him anymore? Did the woman who hadn't had a date in years really want to stop seeing him so she could date other people? None of this made any sense to him at all.

He finally pulled himself up and off the sofa and headed for the second bedroom. As he passed her bedroom, he could hear the sound of her weeping.

The sound of her crying broke his heart even more, but it also deeply confused him. If this was what she really wanted, if she really wanted him out of her life, then why was she crying?

He went on into the second bedroom and sat on the edge of the bed, still stunned by what had happened. What had he missed? He'd tried to be everything she needed him to be. Dammit, what had happened? He finally got up and pulled out the two duffel bags he'd packed to come here. He didn't want to do this. God, he didn't want to pack his things and go home. This was home. Here with Harper was home.

He didn't even think she'd be safe here without him. Somewhere out there was a person who had tried to kill her once. There was no reason to believe he wouldn't try it again, especially without Sam's presence here.

Sam's stomach tightened at the very thought. That, along with his heavy heart, made him pack his things slowly. Maybe he was hoping she'd come back in and stop him. Maybe she'd come in and tell him this was all a big mistake and she was in love with him. But all too soon everything was in the duffel bags and there was nothing more for him to do.

He threw one of the bags over his shoulder and picked up the other one, then he walked down the hallway to her bedroom door. He placed his palm on the door and for several long moments wondered what he could do, what he could say that would change the events of the night. What could he do to make her love him as much as he loved her?

He finally knocked on her door. "Harper, I'm ready to go. Would you at least come out and tell me goodbye?" If she came back out maybe they could have another dialogue about what was happening. Maybe then she could make him understand why this was happening.

"Goodbye, Sam. I'll see you tomorrow at the bakery." Her voice drifted out from behind the closed door.

A little niggle of hope swept through him. So, she hadn't kicked him out of her life all the way. She hadn't mentioned anything about removing him from the job and her words reassured him that hopefully it wasn't going to happen.

So, he'd have his days to work for her and flirt with her and hopefully get back to the way things had been before they'd all changed.

And why had things changed in the first place? It was a question that haunted him as he left her home and headed out to his pickup.

One thing was for sure. He wasn't about to leave her unprotected. He assumed it was perfectly legal for him to park against the curb in front of her house. If she didn't like his presence there, then she would have to call Dallas and have him tell Sam to move along.

Knowing his plan now, he pulled out of her driveway and backed up and then moved against the curb. He'd stay out here for the night...for every night until the bastard who was after her was caught. If he lowered his seat, nobody would see him if he slept in the truck, and the truck's presence would hopefully keep the bad guy away.

He shut off his truck and powered the seat back, giving him plenty of room to get comfortable. He placed his gun in his lap and tried to relax.

His heart still ached with the events of the night, an ache deeper and more painful than he'd ever felt. Tears burned at his eyes. He was a big strong man, but Harper's rejection made him feel weak and emotional.

He'd truly believed that he and Harper were going to have a forever kind of future together. He loved her with a depth and breadth that he knew he would never find again in his life. He'd planned to be with her through eternity and now it was over.

Harper had been crying in her bedroom when he left, which confused him so much. It was as if she hadn't wanted to stop their relationship but some force greater than her was forcing her to break up with him. What on earth could that force be?

She'd appeared to have gotten over the gossip and naysayers. In fact, it had been just like he'd told her it would be... the gossip about the

baker lady and her younger lover had definitely
died down.

He didn't believe it was gossip that had driven
them apart. So, what was it? He began to think
back to exactly when things had changed so dras-
tically between them. It had been after the dinner
at his mother's house. That had been the night
she'd slept alone and things had begun to change.

He frowned thoughtfully. His brothers and
mother had certainly been welcoming to her and
she had seemed to enjoy her time with all of them.

Sure, Lauren had asked her a lot of questions
about being a business owner, but Harper hadn't
seemed to mind the inquiries. In fact, he knew
Harper loved talking business and would want to
help his sister out in any way she could.

However, Lauren had taken Harper outside for a
private conversation. He frowned. He'd thought the
two had merely talked some more about owning
a business, but maybe Lauren had said something
to Harper that had made her pull away from him.

Was it possible? The more he thought about it,
the more he believed this was what might have
happened. Dammit, what had Lauren said to her?
He knew his sister would never want to hurt him,
but sometimes she thought she knew better than
he did what was best for him.

He must have fallen asleep for he jerked awake
suddenly, his heart thundering a million miles a

minute. He grabbed his gun and looked toward her house.

Moonlight drifted down, painting everything in a silvery light. He didn't see anything amiss, but something had awakened him from his sleep. He slid out of his truck quickly and closed the door as softly as possible. He gripped his gun tightly in his hand and every one of his muscles tensed with a fight-or-flight adrenaline.

He checked the front of the house but there was nobody lurking about. He slid around the corner and down the side. He then spun around to the back of the house and again found nobody there. He finally completed his check by coming up the last side.

Nothing. Nobody. He stood by the truck and continued to look around, but there was nothing to give him pause. He finally returned to his truck. As he got back into the seat, from somewhere nearby a dog barked several times. The barks were loud and deep. Maybe that was what had awakened him. He remained awake, looking toward her house for a long time, wanting to make sure she was still safe and sound.

He dozed off and on for the remainder of the night and was finally awakened for good by the sound of Harper's car starting up. He started his truck and when she pulled out of the driveway and headed up the street, he was right behind her.

He followed her to the bakery and watched as

she got out of her car and went inside. She didn't acknowledge his presence in any way but he really hadn't expected her to.

He remained parked outside of the bakery until about seven and then he headed to his house. When he walked through the door there was no sense of homecoming, no warm feelings at all. Home remained Harper's house where he had found such joy, such complete soul-deep contentment.

He took a quick shower and pulled on clean jeans and a white T-shirt. Once he was dressed to work for the day, he got back into his pickup and headed to his sister's place. More than anything, he wanted some answers, and he had a feeling Lauren might be the key to the questions that burned through his brain.

Lauren and Russ lived in a nice ranch house just off Main Street. He never knew when Russ would be home or not as his work hours at the firehouse were not regular ones. However, his car was in the driveway when Sam pulled up.

"Well, isn't this an early morning surprise," Lauren said in delight as she opened her door and ushered him in. "Come on into the kitchen. We were just having coffee and discussing the plans for the reveal party."

"Coffee definitely sounds good to me," he replied. One corner of the living room had boxes stacked up. "Inventory for the new store?"

"Yeah, it's not only taken over my living room

but also my spare bedroom," she replied with a small laugh. "We're trying to get it all into the back room of the store, but so far we still have a lot to move there."

"Hey, Russ," Sam said as he entered the kitchen and saw his brother-in-law seated at the small round wooden table. He was clad in his fire department uniform so Sam knew he was going into work at some point that morning.

"Sam." Russ half rose, but Sam waved him back down. "What's happening?"

"Not much," Sam replied. "What about you?"

"Your sister is trying to work me to death for this new venture of hers," Russ replied. "And if that's not enough, this reveal party she's planning is going to drive me totally insane."

"Oh, don't be a crybaby," Lauren said with a laugh. "Sit, Sam," she added. "I'll pour you a cup of coffee."

"Thanks, sis." Sam sat in the chair opposite Russ.

A moment later Sam had his coffee and Lauren had joined them at the table. "So, how are things going at the shop?" he asked.

"They're going. We still need to unpack a lot of things and get them situated in the space, but we're working on it. I'm hoping we can open in a month."

"At least six to eight weeks," Russ said.

"Oh, pooh, he's the pessimist in this venture," Lauren said with an affectionate look at her husband. Both Russ and Sam laughed. "I want to get the shop taken care of and opened so I can enjoy my pregnancy without stressing about anything else."

"That sounds like a good plan," Sam replied.

"The only person who is stressing in this situation is me," Russ said wryly. "One minute she's bossing me around about the shop and the next minute she's crying because she can't decide how to decorate the nursery."

"Don't remind me," she said. "How are things with you, Sam? I haven't heard from you since we all had dinner at Mom's together."

"Things are going. I'm still working on the bakery."

"I drove by there yesterday and it looks great," Russ said.

"Yeah, it's coming along," Sam replied and then looked at her sister. "Did you enjoy talking to Harper that day?"

"I did," Lauren replied. "She seems very nice and she had a lot of wisdom to impart to me about being a business owner and I really appreciated it."

"Is business all you talked about when you were outside with her?" Sam asked. He eyed his sister carefully. She looked down to her coffee cup and then gazed up at him once again.

"We talked about you a little bit," she replied.

"Really, and what exactly was the conversation?" Sam fought against a sudden tightening in his chest.

"Oh, you know…just silly girl talk." She released a small burst of what he recognized as nervous laughter.

"Before this conversation goes any further, I need to head out for work." Russ drained his coffee cup and stood. Lauren popped up from the table as well. The two kissed, said their goodbyes and then Russ was gone.

"Now, where were we?" Lauren asked as she returned to her seat.

"You were about to tell me what 'just silly girl talk' entailed between you and Harper," Sam said.

"Oh, you know. I asked her if she liked you and I told her you looked like you were really into her."

"And…"

"And she told me that you'd told her that you didn't want children and I might have reminded her that you were young and might not know exactly what you wanted out of life." Lauren released a sigh and her eyes flashed with a touch of defiance. "Okay, I also told her that if she really cared about you, she'd let you go to find somebody your own age."

Sam sat back hard in his chair, his heart falling to the floor. So that was it. It explained everything. After that conversation everything had changed.

"Dammit, Lauren, why would you say something like that to her?"

"I said it because I love you and I want you to find the right woman for you," she said with a slight lift of her chin. "Sam, I was trying to protect you."

"What gives you the right to interfere in my life?"

"Because I'm your big sister and I care about you," Lauren replied, once again raising her chin defensively.

"If you really cared about me, then all you should want is my happiness," he retorted angrily. "Dammit, Lauren, Harper is my happiness, whether you like it or not. I am deeply in love with her and whatever you said to her really screwed things up between us. And now I need to see if I can fix things with her."

"Don't be angry with me, Sam," she said as tears filled her eyes. "I'm sorry I said anything, but I can't stand it if you're angry with me."

He sighed. "Don't cry. It isn't good for the baby." He scooted his chair back and stood. "I love you, Lauren, but I'm pretty upset and disappointed in you right now. I'm not a little boy that you have to protect anymore. I'm a man and I know what I want. I want Harper, and if I manage to fix things with her, then I hope you never do anything like this again."

"I promise," she said, sniffling with emotion. "I just wanted to protect you, Sam."

"I don't need your protection." He leaned down

and kissed her on the forehead. "I'll talk to you later," he said and then strode out of the house and got into his truck. He sat for a moment or two and drew in several deep breaths to steady himself.

Harper had obviously taken Lauren's words to heart. It was the only thing that made any sense. The timing was certainly right. It was after her talk with Lauren that Harper had pulled away from him.

With this new knowledge burning through him, he intended to go and claim his woman. And he believed with all his heart that she was just waiting for him to claim her.

Harper had cried herself to sleep the night before. In fact, she'd cried harder about Sam than when her husband had walked out on her after years of marriage. Saying goodbye to Sam had been the most difficult thing she'd ever done in her life.

She'd been stunned that morning to see his truck parked outside of her house and the fact that he'd probably been there all night long broke her heart all over again. Even though she'd cast him aside, he'd apparently still been on duty to keep her safe.

He'd disappeared at some point while she was in the bakery kitchen preparing things for the day. She assumed he'd be back to work sometime this morning…if he intended to finish the job.

At this point she wasn't sure he'd want to continue working for her. It was going to be difficult going from a loving, romantic relationship to a strictly employer/employee association for both of them.

Still, at nine o'clock she saw his truck pull up outside and she couldn't help the way her heart beat an accelerated rhythm in response. As she watched him get out of his vehicle and wrap the tool belt around his waist, she couldn't help the love for him that buoyed up inside of her. Oh, she loved him so much. He was not only deep in her heart, but he was also deep in her very soul.

Even though it pained her greatly, she felt as if she'd done the right thing in breaking up with him. Eventually he'd find a new love, somebody his own age and that woman would make him far happier than he could ever be with her. But the very thought of him with another woman shot an arrow of pain straight through the center of her heart.

To her surprise, instead of going around back where she assumed he intended to begin working today, he beelined for the front door.

"Hey, Joe… Mark… Larry," he said in greeting to the regulars that were seated at tables inside. He then smiled at her and his eyes shone with a love that weakened her knees and caused a flush of heat to roar through her.

She wanted to scream at him to stop looking at her that way, to stop making her feel the way she did. Oh, she desperately wished she didn't love him as much as she did. It would have been so much easier if she didn't love him.

"'Morning, cutie," he said to her.

She stared at him for a long moment. Had he forgotten that she'd broken up with him the night before? Was he trying to torture her on purpose? "'Morning, Sam, what can I get for you?" She tried to keep all emotion out of her voice and off her face.

"I figured I'd start out the day with one of your awesome cinnamon rolls and a cup of coffee," he replied.

She tried not to look at him as she got his order ready and then he paid. She definitely tried to keep her gaze averted from him as he took a seat at one of the tables closest to the display case.

The next ten minutes or so were sheer agony as Sam ate his roll and drank his coffee with his gaze solely fixed on her. She tried to ignore him but she felt the heat of his gaze on her. When he'd finished eating, he tossed his items and then smiled at her, that full, wonderful smile that caused his dimple to dance in his cheek. "I'm heading out back. I'll see you later." And with that he walked out the front door.

Maybe the breakup hadn't affected him as deeply as it had her. He had appeared perfectly happy this morning going back to his normal routine. Perhaps he was secretly glad that she'd let him go and he hadn't had to break up with her. After all, in the weeks that they had spent together she'd been a tremendous amount of work for him.

First there had been finding Sandy in her backyard, and then there had been the disturbing doll and note. Finally, there had been the attack on her. He'd had to do a lot of emotional cleanups for her during the time they'd been together. Maybe he'd already grown tired of her and just hadn't known how to tell her. The thought somehow broke her heart in a different way.

She pasted a smile on her face for the men who were still inside the bakery and then cleaned off the table where Sam had eaten.

There was a fairly steady influx of traffic throughout the morning and then in the afternoon there was the usual lull. She refilled the display case and was unsurprised when Sam came back in.

"Whew, it's hot out there today," he said.

"You want the usual?" she asked.

"Yeah, except no coffee and instead an iced tea." Once again, he took a seat at the table closest to the counter. "Have you had a good morning?" he asked.

"It was pretty good," she replied. She got the order ready and delivered it to the table.

"Thanks. Sit with me for a few minutes?"

She wanted to sit with him. She didn't want to sit with him. She finally sat across from him. As long as they only talked business, she'd be fine. "What have you done in the back this morning?"

"I've been replacing all the rotten boards and once that's all done, we'll be ready to start the building of the new covered porch," he replied.

"I can't wait to have it done. I'm planning a grand reopening when everything is finished. I'll place flyers all over town and put a big ad in the paper and it will be a totally awesome event." She was nervously rambling, her gaze going all around the room to keep from looking at him.

"Harper, please look at me," he said softly.

She didn't want to look at him, yet she found herself gazing up and into his beautiful green eyes even as she steeled herself for whatever he intended to say to her.

"I stopped by and had coffee with Lauren this morning. She told me about the interesting conversation the two of you had on the front porch." His eyes flashed with a bit of what appeared to be irritation. "Harper, my sister meant well, but she had no right to interfere with my relationship with you. I'm a grown man and I know what I want in life and that's you, Harper. I'm deeply in love with you and you're more than enough to make me happy for the rest of my life."

Oh, God, he was positively breaking her heart. Still, she'd made her decision where he was concerned. It was done. It was over. He might be angry at his sister for what she'd said to her, but Lauren had spoken the honest truth. She'd needed to let Sam go so he could find a love closer to his age.

He had so much going for him and eventually he'd thank her for her decision. Eventually he would find a new love that would truly fulfill him in ways she wouldn't be able to.

"Sam, nothing has changed since last night." Each word ripped at her heart as they fell from her lips. "I still feel like it's best if we both go our own ways. I… I'm ready to move on to date somebody my own age."

His eyes filled with pain and once again she cut her gaze away from him. The last thing she wanted to do was hurt Sam. But once again she reminded herself that someday he would thank her for letting him go. One day she would be just a dim memory in his mind.

"Is there anything I can do…anything I can say to change your mind?" His voice was laced with a deep anguish.

Stay strong, a little voice whispered inside her head. Oh, it was so hard to do when all she really wanted was to fall into his arms and profess the depth of her love for him. Doing the right thing positively sucked.

"There's nothing, Sam. However, I do hope we can maintain a good working relationship, but right now that's all I really want and need from you."

He finally nodded. "Got it." His eyes went dark and shuttered against her.

"Now I need to get some work done." She got up from the table and ten minutes later or so he got up and went back outside.

The day felt ridiculously long. Harper's heart hurt even though she kept assuring herself she had done the right thing. She had never expected things with Sam to last forever. But she'd just always assumed he'd be the one to walk away from her. She'd never dreamed she'd be the one to walk away from him.

At quarter after five when she left the shop, Sam was waiting for her by his truck. "I'll follow you home," he said.

"That's really not necessary," she replied.

"It is for me. I'm not going to leave you all on your own no matter what our personal relationship is like. I haven't forgotten that somebody tried to kill you."

Neither had she. "Thank you, Sam." She raced for her car before he could see the tears that filled her eyes. The fact that he still cared about her safety spoke of the love he had for her…a love she intended not to take as her own no matter how much she wanted to claim it forever.

Chapter 11

Two more days had passed, two more agonizing days where Harper tried to keep a happy smile on her face during business hours while still crying herself to sleep each night.

The house felt so empty without him. She missed having dinner with him then sitting on the sofa and either watching a show or having a playful argument about one silly thing or another. She missed that banter. She just missed him desperately.

The loneliness she'd felt before Sam had entered her life now seemed more immense than ever. It ate at her as the empty evening hours stretched out before her each night.

Sam continued to play bodyguard for her, which

made her sleep better at night. During the days he'd been kind and respectful to her without crossing any boundaries. Still, she felt his love for her every minute that he was around her and as long as he was working for her it would continue to be an exquisite form of torture.

Thankfully today she had a lot of orders going out, so at least through the morning and afternoon she was kept busy with people coming in and out of the business.

It was a gray, overcast day although the forecast didn't call for any rain. Still, the dark clouds reflected Harper's mood. She had a core of sadness inside her that she hoped would eventually ease up and go away but right now it threatened to consume her.

It was during the lull of the afternoon when she was surprised to see Lauren entering the bakery. The woman looked quite pretty in jeans and a pink T-shirt that read Baby On Board with a big arrow pointing to her tummy.

She offered Harper a tentative smile as she approached the display counter. "Hi, Harper."

"Hey, Lauren," Harper replied. "I like your shirt."

"Oh, thanks," Lauren replied.

"So, what can I do for you today?" Why was Sam's sister in here? She'd never been in the bakery before. If Sam had made her come then he'd learn quickly enough that Harper's mind hadn't been changed. Maybe she was here to discuss the gender reveal party.

"My brother has been raving about your cookies so I decided it was past time for me to come in and try them. I'd like a dozen of your oatmeal raisin ones. Then maybe you and I could have a little chat?"

"Okay," Harper agreed, although she couldn't imagine what the two of them had to chat about. Lauren had already been very clear on what she thought about things. "Why don't you have a seat and I'll bring the cookies to you."

Lauren sat at one of the tables. As Harper bagged the cookies to go, she couldn't help but wonder exactly why Lauren was here. What on earth did she have to say to Harper that she hadn't already said? What was done was done, and she couldn't exactly take back what she'd said to Harper that day on the porch.

She brought the bag of cookies to Lauren's table and then sat down opposite the pretty young woman, as the two were the only ones inside at the moment. "What's going on?"

Lauren's features appeared strained and she toyed with the strap on her purse as if nervous. "Harper, I made a big mistake the last time we were together. I should have never gotten involved in your relationship with my brother."

"You just told me how you felt about it all," Harper replied.

"But it wasn't my place to tell you what I thought was best for my brother." She leaned forward. "Harper, I know you broke up with him and if that was because of what I said to you that day, then please reconsider. I've never seen my brother as broken as he's been the last couple of days and it's absolutely killing me to see him that way."

She leaned back in the chair and shook her head. "I had no idea how much he truly loved you. Harper, I had no idea you were the one for him. I should have never, ever interfered. If you can find it in your heart to let him back in, then I know you'd make him a very happy man."

Harper released a weary sigh. "Lauren, I don't intend to change the way things are right now. You were right when you told me it was selfish of me to tie him up romantically. He's a young man and needs to find a nice young woman to date." Saying those words aloud pierced a new arrow into Harper's heart.

Now that she'd made the actual break from Sam, she wasn't going to go backward. The break was destined to happen anyway. Eventually he would want more than she could ever give him.

"I'm so sorry I said anything at all," Lauren said miserably. "It wasn't my place. All I want is for Sam to be happy and now I realize you are… were his true happiness."

"Give yourself a break, Lauren. Your brother is wonderfully handsome and infinitely kind. It won't take him long to find a new girlfriend." Harper was saved from having to say anything else as another customer walked in.

Minutes later Lauren left and Harper breathed a deep sigh of relief. The rest of the afternoon passed slowly. Only a few people came in and Harper found herself having far too much time to think. And the last thing she wanted to think about was Sam.

Instead, she grabbed some paper and a pen and sat behind the display case and began to draw up a potential flyer she'd use for the reopening she was planning. Of course, she knew the place wouldn't be ready for another month or so but at least the task kept her mind busy for a while.

At three thirty Sam surprised her by coming back inside. "Sam, is something wrong?" she asked. It was unusual for him to come into the bakery at this time in the afternoon.

"No…uh, yes. My mom has a doctor's appointment at four and my brother was going to take her, but he got tied up, so now I need to take her."

"Sam, you make your own hours here, and of course if you need to take your mother to a doctor's appointment, I completely understand," she replied. "Is she okay?"

"She's fine. From what she told me, it's just a normal checkup." He frowned. "But that's not the issue."

It was her turn to frown at him. "So, what's the issue?"

"You. I need you to make me a promise." His gaze was intense and his tone was sober.

"What kind of a promise?" she asked in confusion.

"Promise me that you won't leave here today until I come back to follow you home."

"Oh, Sam, it's only a block and a half away. I'm sure I'll be just fine," she protested.

"Please, Harper. Just humor me." His gaze bore into hers intently. "The doctor's appointment shouldn't take too long. Just promise me you'll wait for me here if I'm a little late getting back."

"Okay, I promise," she replied after a moment of hesitation. After all, it wasn't like she had anything to rush home for, so it was an easy promise to make.

"Thank you," he replied in obvious relief. "I'm taking off now but I should be back by five or a few minutes after."

"Take your time. I promise I'll be here when you get back," she assured him. She sighed as he took off. Why did he have to be such a good man? According to Lauren, she'd apparently broken his heart, yet he still cared enough about her to continue to be her bodyguard. He still continued to want to give her her dream as far as the bakery was concerned.

Most men would have left her to her own devices, but not Sam. Not her sweet, sweet Sam. As always, these kinds of thoughts brought the sting of tears to her eyes. Eventually Sam would get over her and someday maybe she would get over Sam, but not today.

She was fifteen minutes from closing up for the day when Celeste Winthrop walked in. Celeste was a very attractive woman with ash-blond hair and big brown eyes. She was dressed in a pair of long white slacks with an emerald green blouse. She wore big gold earrings and a thick gold necklace. She looked cool and chic and made Harper feel positively dowdy in her black slacks and beige blouse.

Celeste was another person who had never been in the bakery before and Harper steeled herself, knowing the woman wasn't after something sweet to eat but rather something else.

"Good afternoon, Celeste. How can I help you today?" Harper greeted the woman.

"Hmm, I'm not sure. I need to look things over," Celeste replied as she stepped up to the display counter.

"Take your time," Harper replied.

The woman walked up and down the display case, looking at all the things inside. She then stopped and looked back up at Harper. "I didn't see Sam's truck outside. Is there trouble in paradise?" she asked with a sly smile.

"No, he's still on the job here," Harper replied.

"Gossip has it that you and Sam are quite cozy with each other."

Harper sighed. So, the woman wasn't here because she'd suddenly gotten hungry for a brownie or a slice of cake. "I'm not sure what you're talking about."

"You know exactly what I'm talking about," Celeste replied. "You know, there aren't that many good men in this town. Surely you could find somebody your own age to date."

"You're way behind in your gossip, Celeste. Sam and I are no longer seeing each other so he's free for you to chase."

Celeste's nose thinned and her eyes narrowed. "I don't chase men…they chase me," she replied haughtily.

"Good for you," Harper replied, tired of the whole conversation. "Now, what can I get for you?"

Celeste swept her gaze over the items and then looked up at Harper. "I thought I was hungry for a little sweet, but I've changed my mind. Thank you anyway." With that the woman turned around and left the bakery.

The woman hadn't come in for a "little sweet," she had come in to get the latest in gossip straight from the horse's mouth. Now she knew there was a green light with Sam, although Harper had a feeling Celeste would have to wait a very long time for Sam to chase her.

Sam wasn't back by closing time and although

she was tempted to go ahead home, she had made a promise to Sam, and she always tried to keep her promises.

She locked the front door and turned off the interior lights and then went back into the kitchen and prepared things for the next morning. Once that was done, she returned to her chair behind the display case and sank down to wait. The bakery was darker than usual because of the gloominess outside that had deepened over the last couple of hours.

Still, she could see well enough that while she waited for Sam, she'd work some more on the paperwork she'd begun earlier.

She pulled out the papers on which she'd drawn a variety of ads to go in the paper and on flyers. She became completely absorbed in the work as she made changes to what she had already done earlier in the day.

She frowned in disgust as she found herself doodling Sam's name over and over again on one of the papers. She was like a love-struck teenager, writing his name repeatedly across the top of an algebra paper.

She'd been sitting there for several minutes when she thought she smelled smoke. Was it coming in from someplace outside? She got up from her chair and sniffed the air. No, it seemed to be coming from the kitchen area.

Had she left something running? Something

that had gotten too hot? She couldn't imagine herself doing something like that, but since she'd broken up with Sam her thoughts had been scattered at best.

She hurried back there. The smell of smoke was much more pronounced in the kitchen and she could actually see it drifting in the air. A quick glance at all the equipment she used let her know nothing was on and running.

What in the heck? She now realized the smoke was coming in beneath the door between the kitchen and the laundry room. She coughed, the dark smoke burning her eyes and lodging in the back of her throat.

She pulled open the door between the two rooms. She gasped and stumbled backward. Fire! Tall flames licked at the wood around the back door. Oh, dear God, her building was on fire.

She slammed the door and raced for the front. She needed to get out and the only way out was through the front door, as the burning back door was no longer an option.

She grabbed her purse from beneath the counter and fumbled to get her keys out. With her keys in hand, she ran to the front door. Before she even tried to unlock it, she saw that the stacks of wood and other building supplies had been moved from the side of the door to directly in front of it. They were all now blocking her way out.

When had that happened? Somebody must have

moved the items when she'd either been back in the kitchen or absorbed with the paperwork. Who had done this?

She didn't have the time to think about who was responsible as a deep sob of panic escaped her. Despite the items in front of it, she unlocked the door and pushed with all her might. The door didn't budge. She shoved against it again. It wouldn't even open an inch, let alone enough for her to get through.

Another fit of coughing overtook her. Dark smoke was growing more and more intense, filling the room with deadly intent. Her lungs ached and tears coursed down her face, both from fear and the smoke.

Once she was finished with the coughing spasm, she went back to the kitchen. The room was dark with smoke and when she placed her hand on the door leading out to the laundry room, the wood was fiery hot.

Oh, God, a new panic roared through her. It was only a matter of minutes before the fire breached the back door and swept into the kitchen.

She ran back to the front door, pushing against it, shoving at it with all her might. "Help me! Please, somebody help me!" she screamed as she banged on the door until she was completely out of breath.

Trapped. She was trapped in a burning building. Who had done this to her? Another round of coughing punished her and a dizziness caused her head to reel.

Her chest felt tight…so tight and it felt as if she couldn't draw in enough oxygen. She sank down to her knees next to the door. She now couldn't see across the room due to the thick smoke that filled the air. Her head reeled as dozens of thoughts moved through her mind as if in slow motion.

Shouldn't she call somebody? Did she have a phone? She needed to call Sam. Sam. Where was Sam? Wasn't he supposed to be here with her? Where was he? Where had he gone? Confusion muddied her thoughts.

She loved him so much. Would she ever see him again? She was so tired. Why was she so sleepy? Maybe she should take a little nap. Things would be better when she woke up.

Another bout of coughing tortured her. Her lungs burned and she realized someplace in the back of her mind that if she didn't do something soon, she was going to die.

"Thank you for taking me today," Sam's mother said to him as they pulled up in her driveway.

"You know I don't mind. I'll walk you inside," he said, then parked and turned off the truck engine. He glanced at the clock on the dashboard. There had been a wait in the doctor's office and it was now a quarter after five. He hoped Harper had kept her promise and was still at the bakery waiting for him.

He was definitely eager to get back there before she gave up on him and decided to go on home without him. He still had a horrible fear for her life. He couldn't get out of his mind the night that she'd been slashed up. He would never forgive himself if anything else happened to her.

Even though she didn't want him anymore, he still wanted to keep her safe from any harm that might come her way. Still, there was nothing worse than unrequited love. He had no idea how long it might take him to recover from Harper. She was and would remain for a very long time a love in his heart and a burn in his very soul.

He'd seen the future with her and he'd loved what he'd visualized for the two of them. Now he had no vision for his future beyond his deep heartbreak.

He walked his mother into the house and she settled into her favorite chair. "I'm glad the doctor gave you a clean bill of health," he said.

"I'm as healthy as a horse," she replied. "Now, where's the remote control?"

It took several minutes for them to find the remote. He kissed her goodbye on her forehead and then he flew out of the house, eager to get back to the bakery.

He knew Lauren had come in to talk to Harper

that afternoon, but apparently his sister hadn't been able to change Harper's mind.

Maybe she really didn't love him, but he swore he felt her love flowing from her when the two of them were in the same room. He believed he saw love in her eyes whenever she gazed at him. How could he possibly convince her that they belonged together forever?

The day had turned preternaturally dark, dark enough that he had to turn his headlights on to drive. As he pulled into the bakery parking lot, he was glad to see Harper's car still parked next to the building. Good, she'd kept her promise and had waited for him.

However, when he stepped out of the car a deep alarm rang through him. Instead of smelling the lingering sweet scent of the bakery, acrid smoke filled the air. The interior of the bakery was dark. He raced up to the door and panic seared through him as he saw the flickering light of flames dancing somewhere in the back of the place.

What the hell? Shock and horror punched into his gut as he saw the building supplies stacked against the front door. He peered inside. It was almost impossible to make anything out through the smoke that filled the place.

Then he saw her… Harper. He could barely see her through the smoke inside. She was curled into an unmoving heap just inside the front door.

"Harper!" He shouted her name and banged on

the door as hard as he could, but she didn't move. Frantic, he pulled out his cell phone and called the emergency number. "Fire…there's a fire at the Sweet Tooth Bakery and Harper is unconscious inside," he yelled.

He put the phone back into his pocket and then banged on the door again in an attempt to rouse Harper. Still she didn't respond.

He was afraid to break the door glass, same with the big picture window next to the door. He was terrified he'd cause the fire to explode outward and burn Harper. And if that didn't happen, he was afraid the glass would shatter all over her and cut her to shreds.

Dammit, he wasn't a fireman. He didn't know what to do in this situation. He just needed to get to her. The one thing he could do was remove the items that were stacked in front of the door. Then, if the door was unlocked, he'd risk opening it to pull her outside.

He had to get her out of there as soon as possible. The smoke in the area she was in was thick and deadly and right now she was unresponsive.

Frantically, he began picking up the wood and tossing it aside. As he worked, he shouted for help. His heart thundered in his chest and tears of fear for her blurred his eyes.

To his surprise and relief, RJ ran over from the tattoo shop and began to help him move the supplies from in front of the door. "What the hell?" RJ exclaimed as he worked to help.

"Somebody did this on purpose," Sam said, his blood boiling with both anger and fear. Had RJ done this and was the big man now trying to play hero? He'd deal with RJ later. Right now, no matter what RJ's motives might be, he was helping.

Was it already too late? Had she succumbed to smoke inhalation? Sam knew that smoke could be the real silent killer in a fire.

Oh, God, she couldn't be dead. She just couldn't be. What would he do without her presence? He'd thought she'd be safe here. He'd believed nobody would try anything while she was inside her bakery. He'd been wrong, so very wrong.

This was all his fault. He should have never left her alone here. He should have never made her promise to stay here to wait for his return. He would never forgive himself if… He couldn't even finish the thought.

Another man Sam didn't even know pitched in to help them move items and before long the doorway was cleared. "If the door is unlocked, I'm going in," Sam said.

"No, man, wait for the firemen to get here," RJ protested. "It's too dangerous."

"She can't wait," Sam cried, even as sirens sounded in the distance. He tried the door. Thankfully it was unlocked. He drew in a deep breath, yanked it all the way open and then stepped inside.

Inside the air was hot and his eyes immediately burned with the smoke. He leaned down next to Harper and scooped her up in his arms. She hung limply and with no response to being moved. A deep sob of despair ripped from him.

RJ opened the door for Sam, and he rushed out into the cooler evening air. Gently he placed Harper on the ground. "Harper… Harper, honey… open your eyes," he said frantically. "Please… please open your eyes."

Suddenly there was chaos all around him. An ambulance pulled up, along with the fire truck and several police cars. Men started spooling out water hoses and carrying them around to the back of the building.

Two EMTs arrived by his side with a gurney. They picked up Harper and then hurried her to the ambulance as a group of onlookers began to gather all around. Before Sam could get his bearings, the ambulance pulled away as Dallas stepped up to Sam's side.

"What happened here, Sam?" Dallas asked tersely.

"Somebody tried to kill Harper." Sam grabbed hold of Dallas's arm. "I don't even know if they succeeded." Sam's eyes blurred with new tears. "God, Dallas, I… I don't even know if she was dead or alive when I pulled her out of there."

"If she's alive they will take good care of her,

Sam," Dallas replied. "Right now, I need some information from you."

Sam quickly told him about his mother's doctor's appointment and the promise Harper had made to him to wait until he returned to go home. "Somebody started a fire at the back of the building and then they used my building supplies to block the front door so she couldn't get out. She was trapped in there. It's all my fault. I should have never left her here all alone." His voice cracked with the depth of his emotion.

Sam's fear for Harper's life and his guilt about the situation nearly cast him to his knees. But he knew Dallas needed as much information as possible to investigate exactly what had happened.

As the lawman continued to question Sam, more people began to gather in the parking lot. All Sam could think about was Harper. How was she doing? Was she going to survive this horrible night? Dear God, had she survived?

Finally, the fire was out. It was Russ who came around to talk to Dallas and Sam about the damage. "The point of ignition was the back door and we believe gasoline was the accelerant. The laundry room is completely burned out, along with the back door area and part of the kitchen. The rest of the interior has probably been badly smoke-damaged but right now it's too hot to go inside to make a full assessment."

"Can I go?" Sam asked Dallas urgently. "I need to get to the hospital to check on Harper."

"Go," Dallas replied. "I'll catch up with you sometime later."

Sam turned and headed to his truck. "Hey, Sam." Joe Rogers approached him. "Is Harper all right?"

"I don't know. I'm heading to the hospital now to find out," Sam replied. He frowned as he gazed at the man who was one of Harper's regulars.

Was that soot across Joe's forehead? How had the man gotten soot on his face? He hadn't been anywhere near the fire. And his hair appeared a slightly lighter color, as if it was dusted with ash. Sure, there had been some ash flying in the air as a result of the fire, but nobody had been here long enough to get soot and ash all over them.

Sam's heart began beating a different kind of a rhythm. Joe? Was it possible? Did he have some sort of an obsession with Harper? An obsession that had turned deadly?

"Excuse me for a minute, Joe," Sam said. He ran back to where Dallas was now talking to RJ. "I think it's Joe… Joe Rogers," he said to Dallas urgently. "He's got soot on his face and, Dallas, he was nowhere near the fire. You need to check him out, I think you need to arrest him, Dallas. I believe he set the fire and that's how he got the soot on his forehead. I think he's the one who attacked Harper."

Sam didn't wait but instead turned around, ran past Joe and got into his truck. Joe. That bastard. If what Sam thought was true, then hopefully Dallas would take care of him.

Right now, the only thing on Sam's mind was Harper. It was only in the privacy of his truck that he allowed frightened tears to course down his cheeks.

Harper... Harper, her name ripped through him. She had to be okay. The more he thought about it, the more he was now convinced Joe had been her attacker. Had Joe committed murder tonight? The very thought tore through him. Oh, God, he prayed not.

Right now, he didn't care if he and Harper ever got back together again. She just needed to be alive. She needed to be running her bakery and laughing and smiling with customers. Dammit, she had to be alive.

He drove as fast as possible and finally reached the hospital. He parked and flew out of his truck and then he raced into the emergency waiting room.

Sherry Alyers, a woman he'd dated years before, sat behind the desk. "Sherry, Harper Brennan was just brought in by ambulance. Would you let the doctor know I'm here and need to know her condition as soon as possible?"

"I'll let him know." She got up from her chair

and disappeared behind a door right behind the desk.

Sam began to pace the floor, his heart beating so fast he felt short of breath. All he really needed to hear was that she was okay. He just needed to see her for a minute to assure himself she was really going to survive this horrendous night.

"The doctor said he'll be out to speak to you when he can," Sherry said as she returned to her desk.

"Thanks, Sherry."

The minutes ticked by…long minutes that turned into an hour. Sam finally sat. What was taking so long? Was it a good sign that the doctor hadn't come out to talk to him yet? Or was it a very bad sign?

Another hour passed and Dallas arrived. "Any word yet?" he asked.

"No…nothing."

Dallas sank down in the chair next to Sam. "You were right about Joe. I found two gas cans in his car and he confessed to everything. Seems he couldn't stand seeing Harper dating a younger man."

"That bastard," Sam exclaimed, rich anger taking the place of worry for just a moment.

"Wait, there's more," Dallas said. "He not only confessed to attacking her and setting the fire, but he also copped to killing his wife years ago and burying her in his barn. According to him, his wife was leaving him for a much younger man. The night she was leaving they got into a fight and she fell and hit her head. Harper seeing you apparently triggered him."

"That son of a bitch," Sam said angrily. "So, he's now in jail?"

"Yes, and he'll be charged with enough crimes to keep him locked up for a very long time. I've got men out at his place right now digging up his barn floor." Dallas stood. "Let me go see if I can find out some information for you." He walked up to the desk and Sherry then buzzed him in through the large double doors that said Emergency Room.

Sam tried to digest everything Dallas had just shared about Joe. He'd been…just a regular Joe, who came into the bakery for coffee and a cinnamon roll most mornings. But apparently, he hadn't been just a regular Joe at all. He'd been a man with secrets and a twisted darkness inside him that had caused him to want Harper dead like the wife who had apparently betrayed him.

Dallas finally returned with Dr. Alex Erickson by his side. Sam jumped up from his chair. "How is she?" he immediately asked Alex.

"She's stable," Alex replied. Sam nearly fell to the floor in relief. "Needless to say, she's suffered from smoke inhalation," Alex continued. "I've got her on oxygen and I sedated her. We've run some tests and I don't believe her lungs have been damaged but we'll check again in another day or so."

"Can I see her?" Sam asked.

"Sam, she's sleeping. She won't even know you're there," Alex replied.

"I... I just need to see her for a minute," Sam replied. "Please."

"I don't want her disturbed in any way," Alex said firmly. "She's in room 105."

"Thanks." Sam turned and headed down the hallway that held the patient rooms.

When he reached her room, he stepped just inside the door and his heart squeezed tight. She looked so small in the hospital bed. She had an IV in her arm and an oxygen tube down her throat.

More than anything he wanted to curl up on the bed with her and draw her into his arms. He wanted to keep her from harm, from heartache for the rest of her life.

He remained in the doorway for several minutes, watching the reassuring sight of her chest rise and fall. Thank God she was okay. However, she was going to be devastated when she learned of all the damage in the bakery.

He would rebuild it for her. Whatever it took, if she allowed him, he would work hard for her to get the bakery up and running again.

Finally, he left the doorway, knowing there was nothing more he could do for her tonight. Night had fallen and finally the dark clouds had moved out, revealing a sky full of bright stars.

He remained just sitting in his truck for long

moments. It was finally over. He would no longer have to play bodyguard for her anymore. He'd failed miserably at the job anyway.

Still, with Joe in jail she would now be safe to live her life to the fullest without any more fear. Without him. She didn't want him anymore. Now that the danger to her had passed, his heartbreak roared through him harder and more painful than ever.

If she wanted, he'd work to give her a dream bakery, but he'd just be the carpenter who worked for her and nothing more. He had to face the fact, and the fact was that he and Harper weren't going to have a future together.

Chapter 12

On the third morning in the hospital, Harper awakened before the sun came up and was grateful that she no longer had the oxygen tube in and the IV was out.

For the past two days she'd been lightly sedated and had drifted in and out of sleep. She'd had no visitors as the doctors had wanted her to rest without interruption.

But she had suffered from nightmares of smoke and fire that had often jerked her from her sleep gasping and panicked. Still, the doctors had been very protective of her rest and recovery time.

The only people she had seen during the past two days were the doctors and nurses who came in to check on her. She'd been told she'd suffered from smoke inhalation, but thankfully no long-term damage had been done.

However, she knew the bakery was probably in ruins. She hadn't asked anyone about it, hadn't even wanted to think about it until this morning.

She remembered the flames and the smoke, and she remembered that she'd been trapped, but she had no memory of getting out of the bakery and to the hospital.

Sam. Thoughts of him caused tears to immediately fill her eyes. She'd pushed him out of her life…her bakery was in ruins and this morning she felt utterly hopeless and more alone than she'd ever felt.

She dozed off and on until breakfast was delivered. She was grateful for the hot coffee but picked listlessly at the scrambled eggs and hash browns. She really wasn't hungry.

Soon after her breakfast tray was taken away, Dallas walked into her room. "Hey, Harper. How are you feeling this morning?" He sank down in the chair next to her bed.

"I'm okay." Her throat was scratchy and her voice was slightly hoarse, but the doctors had assured her this would eventually pass.

"I need to ask you some questions. Do you feel up to it?" Dallas asked.

She nodded affirmatively. "That would be fine, and then I have some questions for you."

"Basically, I need you to tell me exactly how

things went down in the bakery on the day of the fire," Dallas said.

Harper began to tell him what had happened from the moment she'd smelled smoke. She went through her frantic efforts to shove open the door barricaded with the building supplies until she had apparently fallen unconscious from the smoke. "I don't know how I got out of the bakery. Maybe you could answer that question for me."

"Sam got you out. According to a few witnesses, he worked like a wild animal to move the things from in front of the door and then went in and carried you out."

Her heart squeezed tight. Of course, Sam had saved her...her sweet Sam. Only he wasn't hers anymore. "After you were taken away in the ambulance, Sam noticed something odd about Joe," Dallas continued.

She looked at Dallas in surprise. "Joe... Joe Rogers?"

"Yes. Sam noticed he had some soot on his face and drew it to my attention. Upon further investigation I discovered two empty gas cans in Joe's car. He set the fire, Harper. He was the person who was trying to kill you."

Harper stared at him in stunned surprise. "But wh-why?"

As Dallas told her about Joe, she was utterly shocked by the news. It was so difficult to believe that the man who had been a friendly regular customer had harbored so many secrets and so much hatred toward her.

"According to what Joe told me, he had feelings for you and had just been waiting for the perfect time to ask you out, but then you started seeing Sam and that triggered him and turned his affection into hatred of you."

"It's all just so hard to believe. I would have never guessed that Joe was behind the attacks on me," she replied. "So, tell me what state the bakery is in." She steeled herself for his response. Had it burned down to the ground? Was it nothing more than charred rubble now?

"The back of the building was badly burned, but they got the fire out before it really got too far into the kitchen. However, the whole thing has been smoke-damaged," Dallas said.

She supposed she should be glad that it was no worse than it was, but it definitely sounded fairly dismal. At least she had insurance that should take care of most of it, but it would probably be months and months before she could get it back up and running again.

To her surprise tears began to well up in her eyes once more. She released an embarrassed laugh and reached out for a tissue from the box on her bedside table. "I'm sorry, I seem to be a bit weepy today." She swiped at her eyes with the tissue.

"Don't apologize," Dallas said. "You've been

through quite an ordeal, Harper, and you're lucky to be alive right now."

"I'm very lucky," she agreed faintly. But right now, she didn't feel so lucky. Everything felt so overwhelming. She had a burned-out building with heavy smoke damage. She would have to start a cleanup and then a rebuild. And once again she was facing everything alone.

"Do you have any other questions for me?" Dallas asked.

She had a million questions. Was Sam okay? Had he even tried to come and see her? Or had his interest in her…had his love for her already waned?

Of course, she didn't ask any of those questions. In reality she no longer had the right to ask anything about Sam, except one. And that one suddenly thundered in her chest.

"Was Sam hurt while getting me out?"

"No, not at all," Dallas replied.

She released the breath she hadn't realized she'd been holding. Thank God he hadn't been hurt. "I guess that's all the questions I have for you right now," she said.

Once again, she felt the press of hot tears burning her eyes. What on earth was wrong with her? She was a strong woman. She'd faced adversity before. However, everything right now felt bigger than anything she'd ever dealt with before.

"Harper, if you think of any more questions for me, don't hesitate to call me," Dallas said.

"Thank you, Dallas," she replied.

Dallas left and soon after that Dr. Ralph Reeves came into her room. The older man had been Harper's personal doctor whenever she'd needed one in the past. He was a kind, quiet man who treated his patients with kindness and respect.

"How is my patient doing today?" he asked with a warm smile as he sat in the chair Dallas had recently vacated.

"My throat is still a little scratchy, but other than that I'm feeling fine," she replied.

"I think you're well enough to go home today," Dr. Reeves said. "How do you feel about that?"

"I feel good about it," she replied.

"The only way I'll let you go today is if you promise to rest at home for at least a couple of days," Dr. Reeves said. "I know you'll feel like you need to jump into things, especially considering the state of your place of business, however it's important that you give yourself time to finish healing. So, can you promise me that you'll take things slowly and do a lot of nothing for a while?"

"I can promise you that," she agreed. It was actually an easy promise to make. She was exhausted…utterly drained. All she wanted to do now was go home and rest comfortably in her own bed. Anything that needed to be done at the bakery could wait for a couple of days for her to get her energy back.

"Then I'll get your paperwork all ready and you should be set to leave within the hour." Dr. Reeves stood and gave her a kind smile. "Please take good care of yourself, Harper."

"I plan to. Thank you, Dr. Reeves." It was only minutes after the doctor had left her room that she realized she had a problem. Her car wasn't here and she had no idea who to call to take her home.

Millsville was a very small town. There were no taxis on standby or Uber services available to whisk people from place to place. The women she'd once considered her close friends were both at work and in any case, she would be reluctant to call them. She wasn't in the mood to hear any 'I told you sos' from anybody.

She scarcely had time to think as the nurse, Amber James, came into her room. She carried what appeared to be a pair of Harper's jeans and one of her blue blouses. She also had a small paper bag and Harper's purse in hand.

"Somebody brought in some clean clothes for you to put on. We bagged the clothing you came in wearing because of their intense smoke smell. And if you want to take a quick shower before you put on the clean clothes, I'll wait for you."

"Oh, I'd love a quick shower," Harper replied. She could smell the smoke that lingered in her hair and felt it wafting from her body. She couldn't wait to feel clean again.

"Chief Calloway also brought your purse in. He thought you might need it. We tried to wipe it down to get most of the soot and ashes off it."

"That was very nice of him and I really appreciate you wiping it down," Harper replied. Thank goodness Dallas had realized she'd need her purse when she was discharged and got home. Despite the wipe-down that had been done on it, the purse was still smoke-darkened. Once she got her personal items from it, it would need to be thrown away.

Minutes later she stood beneath a warm spray of water, lathering her hair with the little bottle of shampoo and washing herself with the small bar of soap that had been provided to her. It felt good to finally wash the smoke smell down the drain.

Sam had brought her the clothes. There was no other answer in her mind. He still had a key to her house and he was thoughtful enough to think about providing her something clean to go home in. Once again, her heart squeezed tight as she thought of him and new tears mingled with the shower spray.

Once her shower was finished and as she dressed, her problem returned to her head. How was she going to get home? She needed to figure something out quickly. She finished dressing and sat on the edge of her bed to await her discharge.

While she was contemplating her problem *he*

walked in the door. Sam. For a moment her breath caught in her throat. His face appeared drawn and the bright sparkle in his eyes was dimmed, as if he was incredibly tired. But the smile he offered her was one that warmed her despite their current circumstances.

"I heard that you were going home today and I was wondering if you needed a ride," he said.

"H-how did you know?" she asked.

"I have to confess, I've kind of been a pain in everyone's butt here for the last couple of days. I've been hanging out and asking about you. I came earlier to see if I could visit you today, but they told me to wait until the doctor came in to see you. Dr. Reece came to the waiting room and told me that I could see you and that you were being released. So…do you need a ride home?"

"Would you mind?" Even though this felt awkward, she was grateful he'd showed up.

He smiled once again. "Of course, I wouldn't mind."

"I…uh… I'm just waiting for my discharge papers," she explained.

"Then I'll wait with you." He sat in the chair at the foot of the bed. "How are you feeling?"

"Better than the last time you saw me." She didn't want to look at him. She didn't want to let his beautiful eyes, his caring gaze into her heart.

"Does your throat hurt?" he asked curiously. "You're definitely a bit hoarse."

"It hurts a little bit, but not much," she replied. She finally looked at him. "Thank you, Sam. Thank you for saving my life."

The smile on his face fell and his eyes darkened. "God, Harper, when I saw you in the bakery that was filled with so much smoke, and you were on the floor and not moving at all, I... I thought you were gone." His voice cracked a bit and he averted his gaze from her.

"And all I could think about was that it was all my fault. I was the one who made you promise to stay in the bakery. If I hadn't done that, then maybe the fire wouldn't have happened and you wouldn't have been trapped." His voice sounded tortured with guilt.

"Sam, look at me." He slowly raised his gaze back up to her. "You are not responsible for what happened. Joe was. He was the one who set the fire and if it hadn't happened when it did, then it would have happened on another day. You have no reason to feel guilty about anything that happened that night."

He released a deep sigh. "I'm just so sorry about everything."

Amber came back into the room with some paperwork in her hand as she pushed a wheelchair. She handed the papers to Harper, along with a bright smile. "Okay, Harper. You're all set and you're free to leave."

"The bright side of all this is that it's finally

over. The bad guy is in jail and I'm still alive," she said.

"Thank God for that," he replied.

"And thank you for all your care, Amber," Harper said as she stood and then sat in the wheel-chair. She felt silly sitting in the chair, but knew it was protocol when leaving the hospital.

"It was my pleasure," Amber replied.

"I'll just go pull my truck up," Sam said and then left the room.

Amber pushed her down the hallway and out the emergency room door where Sam had arrived at the curb. "Now, take care of yourself and remember to get plenty of rest," Amber said.

"I will," Harper replied. "Thanks again, Amber."

Sam got out of his truck and helped Harper into the passenger seat. "All ready?" he asked once he was behind the steering wheel.

"Ready," she agreed as she tightened her seat belt. As always, just being around Sam broke her heart all over again. The scent of his cologne smelled like love. His body warmth that wafted toward her made her want to curl up in his arms and never leave.

She drew in a deep breath and released it slowly as he started the truck engine. "Before you take me home, would you please take me to the bakery?" Her heart was already hurting because of Sam.

Maybe it was the right time to get all the hurt out of the way today.

Sam looked at her in surprise. "Are you sure you're up to that right now? I thought your discharge instructions were for you to go home and get plenty of rest."

"I don't intend to do anything at the bakery. I... I just need to see it."

Even though he didn't think it was a good idea, he turned down the street that would take them to the burned-out business. His heart hurt for what she was about to see. He knew she would be devastated by the damage.

He loved her so much and he wished he could protect her from the heartache he knew she would feel. But he couldn't protect her.

He pulled up in front of the bakery. From this vantage point the damage wasn't really visible. "I need to get out," she said. "Do you have time?"

He hesitated a moment and then nodded. "I have all the time you need."

She cast him a grateful smile and then opened the truck door. He quickly got out of the truck and hurried around to meet her.

He frowned as she pulled her set of keys from her purse. He hadn't realized she meant to go inside. Oh, this was going to be so tough on her. He was just glad he would be with her when she got her first glimpse of all the damage. He'd hate for her to face it all alone.

She unlocked the door and pushed it open. Immediately the smell of smoke and wet wood drifted out to greet them. She paused for a long moment and then stepped inside with him at her heels.

The walls inside were dark with smoke damage and the tables and counters were covered with a thin layer of soot. She said nothing as she walked through to the kitchen area where the laundry room was nothing more than charred wood. The back door was completely burned out, leaving a gaping hole in the building.

She stepped out of it and walked to the center of the backyard, her gaze on the back of the bakery. He felt her tears before she began to shed them, silent tears that slowly trekked down her cheeks.

"Harper, we'll clean it…and we'll rebuild it," he said fervently. "We'll make it better than ever." He wanted to do something…to say anything that would stop her from crying, stop her from hurting.

"I knew it was going to be bad, but I still hadn't realized just how bad it was going to be," she said amid her tears.

"I swear, Harper, I'll be right by your side to set this all right." He couldn't help himself. He couldn't just stand there and watch her cry all alone.

He reached out for her and she came willingly

into his arms. She buried her face in the front of his T-shirt and began to cry in earnest.

He held her tight, rubbing one hand up and down her back in an effort to soothe her. At the same time, he whispered words of encouragement, of caring and of love into her ear.

She finally stopped crying but remained in his arms. "Oh, Sam, why do you have to be so wonderful?" she asked softly.

He released a small laugh. "I'm not consciously trying to be wonderful. I just… I just love you, Harper."

She completely stilled and then she finally raised her head and gazed up at him. "I love you, too."

His heart lifted at her words even as confusion filled him. "Then why did you send me away from you?"

She stepped out of his arms and stared back at the bakery. "I tried to do the right thing for you." She turned and looked at him and, in her eyes, he saw a combination of confusion and sadness and love.

"What do you mean?" he asked.

"I tried to send you away so you could find a woman your own age, so you could have a family if you wanted one. I sent you away because I'll never really be enough for you."

He stared at her for a long moment. "I hate him," he finally said.

She looked at him in confusion. "Who?"

"Your ex-husband, the man who made you believe you aren't enough. I think he crippled you, Harper. He made you believe you weren't pretty enough or smart enough to hold a man's attention. I wish you could see yourself through my eyes because I think you're a real catch."

She gazed at him for several moments and in those moments, he found it impossible to read her. "Sam, I'm very set in my ways," she finally said.

He smiled at her. "The good news is that I'm very set in your ways, too." He was rewarded with her small burst of laughter. Encouraged by her response, he continued. "The good thing is you're a woman young at heart and I'm an older man at heart. That makes us absolutely perfect for each other."

"You know occasionally I have…uh…my own personal summers," she said.

"You mean your hot flashes," he replied. "They don't last long and besides, I'm not surprised you're having them because I find you a very hot woman."

He'd been hoping she would laugh again, but instead she frowned. "Sam, I don't want to be the one to keep you from anything you might want in your life."

"Don't you get it? Harper, all I want is to spend my life with you. I never thought marriage would be for me until I met you. Harper, I want to marry you. I want to cook and eat meals with you, I want to watch movies with you and have you in my arms when I go to sleep for the night. I want you, Harper, for the rest of my life."

"I'm so afraid of hurting you," she replied softly. "I do love you, Sam. I love you with all my heart and soul, but I'm so afraid of hurting you."

"Baby, the only way you'll hurt me is if for some crazy reason you keep your love away from me. Harper, surely the events of the last few days has proven to you that life is far too short not to be happy. You have to trust me. You have to trust in us. If I'm your happiness as you are mine, then choose me. Build a life with me."

Tears began to seep from her eyes once again and his heart crashed to the ground. He had no more he could say to her, no more to give to her to make her see they belonged together.

"No matter what our personal relationship is, if you allow me then I'll rebuild your bakery," he finally said. "I'll give you your dream where it's concerned. That, I can promise you."

"Forget about the bakery," she said. She swiped her tears from her cheeks and offered him a small smile. "Sam, you are one tenacious man. And I want you," she replied, her eyes suddenly shining brilliantly. "I choose you, Sam."

He didn't give her a chance to say anything more. He reached out, drew her into his arms and kissed her with all the love he had in his heart for her.

She returned his kiss, leaning into him as she wrapped her arms around his neck. When the kiss finally ended, he smiled at her. "That's my girl," he said.

She stepped away from him and grabbed his hand. "Come on, Sam. Let's go home."

His heart roared with happiness. Home. Home with Harper. He couldn't wait for his future with her to begin.

Epilogue

Harper sank down in a folding chair and released a deep, tired sigh. All around her people were working to scrub clean the walls inside the bakery.

It had been almost two weeks since the fire. When she and Sam had begun the cleanup work two days ago, Harper had been stunned by the amount of people who had shown up to help. Not only had her regular customers come in to work, but also townspeople she'd never even met came in to assist her.

The work on the outside had also begun. Even though it would take a while for the insurance issue to all get settled, Sam and his brothers had been tearing out the burned wood and replacing it.

Despite the fire and the destruction of her property it had caused, Harper had never been happier in her entire life. Sam had moved back in and every night she fell asleep in his arms.

She was surprised to realize there were far more people who didn't have a problem with their relationship than the few vocal people who did. The naysayers no longer bothered her and they had never bothered Sam and that was all that was important.

Sam was not only planning their first trip together, but he was also encouraging her to plan a wedding. He insisted he wouldn't be completely happy until they were married and even though she had never thought she'd get married again, she was positively thrilled by the idea of becoming Sam's wife.

He had brought so much change to her life, wonderful changes that excited her and inspired her. Life really was too short not to reach out for happiness and love when it came your way.

Fifteen minutes later Harper was thanking people and telling them goodbye as closing time arrived. As the place emptied out, Sam came through from the back.

His white T-shirt was filthy and soot streaked his face. He'd never looked as handsome to her. "Hi, cutie," he said to her once the last person had left. He drew her into his arms. "How's my best girl?"

"Good," she replied. "I'll be better if I get a kiss from my best guy."

His eyes twinkled brightly. "I think I can do

that." He leaned down and captured her lips with his in a kiss of infinite caring and endless love.

Nobody could predict the future, but Harper knew her future was with the handsome hunk who had unexpectedly walked into her life and had filled it with an abundance of love. Her sweet, sweet Sam had made her life complete.

Dallas sat in his office alone. He leaned back in his chair and rubbed his tired eyes. It was after midnight, he should be home in bed, but lately he'd been reluctant to go to sleep. When he did finally fall asleep, he suffered from horrendous nightmares.

In those bad dreams, despite their mouths being sewn shut, Sandy and Cindy cried and screamed for justice. Despite being tied to poles, they chased him through a dark landscape until he woke up panicked and out of breath.

So far, the killer hadn't made any mistakes. He'd been organized and controlled, both qualities that made him more dangerous and harder to find than the garden-variety messy killer.

As yet, he'd found no motive in Cindy's or Sandy's personal lives that would explain their murders. It appeared the killer had picked his victims randomly, as well as the places he'd left their bodies.

Dallas leaned forward once again and stared down at the thick pile of notes from interviews he and his officers had conducted over the past two months. Nothing. There was absolutely nothing in those papers to give him a clue as to who he was chasing. Right now, he was just chasing his own damned tail.

He knew people were frightened in his town and it killed him that so far, he'd been able to do nothing about it. Right now, Millsville was a playground for a killer who turned young women into human scarecrows. The thing that scared him the most was that it was going to take more murders before the killer finally got sloppy and left a real clue behind.

He couldn't stand the thought of another young woman losing her life. But at the moment he felt like he was just holding his breath until another murder occurred.

* * * * *

Don't miss Carla Cassidy's previous title
in The Scarecrow Murders:

Killer in the Heartland

Other titles include:

The Last Cowboy Standing
The Cowboy's Targeted Bride
Cowboy's Vow to Protect

Available now from
Harlequin Romantic Suspense

Get 4 FREE REWARDS!

We'll send you 2 FREE Books plus 2 FREE Mystery Gifts.

FREE
Value Over
$20

Both the **Harlequin Intrigue®** and **Harlequin® Romantic Suspense** series feature compelling novels filled with heart-racing action-packed romance that will keep you on the edge of your seat.

YES! Please send me 2 FREE novels from the Harlequin Intrigue or Harlequin Romantic Suspense series and my 2 FREE gifts (gifts are worth about $10 retail). After receiving them, if I don't wish to receive any more books, I can return the shipping statement marked "cancel." If I don't cancel, I will receive 6 brand-new Harlequin Intrigue Larger-Print books every month and be billed just $6.49 each in the U.S. or $6.99 each in Canada, a savings of at least 13% off the cover price, or 4 brand-new Harlequin Romantic Suspense books every month and be billed just $5.49 each in the U.S. or $6.24 each in Canada, a savings of at least 12% off the cover price. It's quite a bargain! Shipping and handling is just 50¢ per book in the U.S. and $1.25 per book in Canada.* I understand that accepting the 2 free books and gifts places me under no obligation to buy anything. I can always return a shipment and cancel at any time by calling the number below. The free books and gifts are mine to keep no matter what I decide.

Choose one: ☐ **Harlequin Intrigue**
Larger-Print
(199/399 HDN GRJK)

☐ **Harlequin Romantic Suspense**
(240/340 HDN GRJK)

Name (please print)

Address   Apt. #

City   State/Province   Zip/Postal Code

Email: Please check this box ☐ if you would like to receive newsletters and promotional emails from Harlequin Enterprises ULC and its affiliates. You can unsubscribe anytime.

Mail to the **Harlequin Reader Service:**
IN U.S.A.: P.O. Box 1341, Buffalo, NY 14240-8531
IN CANADA: P.O. Box 603, Fort Erie, Ontario L2A 5X3

Want to try 2 free books from another series? Call 1-800-873-8635 or visit www.ReaderService.com.

*Terms and prices subject to change without notice. Prices do not include sales taxes, which will be charged (if applicable) based on your state or country of residence. Canadian residents will be charged applicable taxes. Offer not valid in Quebec. This offer is limited to one order per household. Books received may not be as shown. Not valid for current subscribers to the Harlequin Intrigue or Harlequin Romantic Suspense series. All orders subject to approval. Credit or debit balances in a customer's account(s) may be offset by any other outstanding balance owed by or to the customer. Please allow 4 to 6 weeks for delivery. Offer available while quantities last.

Your Privacy—Your information is being collected by Harlequin Enterprises ULC, operating as Harlequin Reader Service. For a complete summary of the information we collect, how we use this information and to whom it is disclosed, please visit our privacy notice located at corporate.harlequin.com/privacy-notice. From time to time we may also exchange your personal information with reputable third parties. If you wish to opt out of this sharing of your personal information, please visit readerservice.com/consumerschoice or call 1-800-873-8635. **Notice to California Residents**—Under California law, you have specific rights to control and access your data. For more information on these rights and how to exercise them, visit corporate.harlequin.com/california-privacy.

HIHRS22R3

HARLEQUIN
PLUS

Announcing a **BRAND-NEW**
multimedia subscription service
for romance fans like you!

Read, Watch and Play.

Experience the easiest way to get
the romance content you crave.

Start your **FREE 7 DAY TRIAL** at
<u>www.harlequinplus.com/freetrial</u>.